GUSTAV

T0022821

THE SHORT STORIES OF GUSTAV MEYRINK

VOLUME I (THE OPAL AND OTHER STORIES)

translated and with an Introduction by Maurice Raraty
and with
Wetherglobin translated by Mike Mitchell

Dedalus

Supported using public funding by
**ARTS COUNCIL
ENGLAND**

Published in the UK by Dedalus Ltd
24-26, St Judith's Lane, Sawtry, Cambs PE28 5XE
info@dedalusbooks.com
www.dedalusbooks.com

ISBN printed book: 978 1 915568 04 5
ISBN ebook: 978 1 907650 96 3

Dedalus is distributed in the USA & Canada by SCB Distributors
15608 South New Century Drive, Gardena, CA 90248
info@scbdistributors.com   www.scbdistributors.com

Dedalus is distributed in Australia by Peribo Pty Ltd
58, Beaumont Road, Mount Kuring-gai, N. S. W. 2080
info@peribo.com.au   www.peribo.com.au

Publishing History
First published by Dedalus in 1994 as The Opal (and other stories)
Republished in 2023 as The Short Stories of Gustav Meyrink Volume I

Translation copyright © Dedalus 1994

The right of Maurice Raraty and Mike Mitchell to be identified as the
translators of this work has been asserted by them in accordance with the
Copyright, Designs and Patents Act, 1988.

Printed and bound in the UK by Clays, Ecograf S.p.A.
Typeset by Marie Lane

Contents

All translations are by Maurice Raraty unless
otherwise specified

INTRODUCTION

All the stories translated here are taken from a collection first published under the title *Des deutschen Spießers Wunderhorn* in 1913. It is an odd and characteristically barbed title. In the first place it is intended to remind us of *Des Knaben Wunderhorn* ('The Boy's Magic Horn'), a collection of verses put together by the German Romantic poets Achim von Arnim and Clemens Brentano in 1806/8, and so embedded in the popular consciousness as to have become an indispensable part of any sentimental German-speaker's literary 'heritage'. In Meyrink's terms however it also calls to mind by implication the heritage of the 'Spießer', that is, the 'Philistine', the conventional, correct bourgeois of few literary pretensions, who possesses the book only because it is the proper thing to have in one's domestic library.

And yet of course the stories he is about to unfold are anything but the proper thing to have in such circumstances, with their withering attacks upon the pillars of order, of upright respectability and authority: the pompous, empty-headed Wilhelminian military officer, the self-important medical man or the bureaucratic government official, in short, all 'normal' assumptions about comfortable and civilised living. Instead, he presents an alternative, subversive underworld of mysterious uncertainties, inexplicable by the rational means of Western thought. It is a world of absurdities, of dreams and nightmares of occult oriental magic, of the horrors that lie beneath the surface, which may be raised through the extension of reality by means of a little imagination.

Meyrink's style and use of language is similarly suitably allusive, extremely spare, but consequently all the more vivid in the occasional multiplicity of underlying significances and implications. Occasionally (as in *Blamol*, for instance), he indulges in an extended joke, turning the whole world upside-down into an undersea parody of reality.

Prior to the publication of *Des deutschen Spießers Wunderhorn* many of these tales had appeared in one or other of three smaller collections: *Der heiße Soldat und andere Geschichten* (1903); *Orchideen, Sonderbare Geschichten* (1904), and *Das Wachsfigurenkabinett, Sonderbare Geschichten* (1907). Even before this however most of these 'strange stories' were issued as contributions to the famous satirical weekly *Simplicissimus* between October 1901 and July 1908. *Der heiße Soldat* indeed, the title story of the first collection (translated here, with suitable ambiguity, as *The Ardent Soldier*), was Meyrink's very first published work. In keeping with the bizarre nature of some of the stories, it too gave his literary career a curious start, for when it was first received at the offices of *Simplicissimus* it was consigned to the wastepaper basket by a sub-editor of the paper, who considered it to be the work of a 'madman', and it was only by chance that it was picked out again on the point of his walking stick by the writer Ludwig Thoma, idly rummaging about. He however on reading it recognised it as a work of 'genius', had it printed, and commissioned more.

The Ardent Soldier, though it is the earliest story to come from Meyrink's pen, is already written in characteristic style, and contains most of the themes of his subsequent work. All these tales however predate the period of Meyrink's greatest (but relatively short-lived) fame, generated by the publication of his best-known novel *The Golem* in 1915.

Meyrink did not set out to be a writer. Born in 1868, he was the illegitimate son of a Viennese actress, Maria Meyer (he changed his name to Meyrink partly on the grounds of a supposed family link to an ancient Bavarian noble line called Meyerinck, but also because he felt he 'shared the name of Meyer with too many people') and a Württemberg government minister, the impressively named Gottlob Karl Freiherr Varnbühler von und zu Hemmingen, who generously provided for his son a sum of money in trust that was to enable him in 1889 on attaining his majority to set up as a banker in Prague, in association with the nephew of the poet Christian Morgenstern.

The House of Meyer & Morgenstern was anything but conventional: Meyer, the dandy, with new access to money, determinedly cut a dash with his clothes and his accessories, always in the most modern fashion. He kept white mice and other more exotic pets, by all reports quite deliberately in order to shock and provoke the worthy citizens of Prague. His unorthodox background made him already conscious of his position as an 'outsider', beyond the limits of conventional bourgeois society, and he seemed determined to live up to it. By nature essentially an intro-vert, he countered the tendency by displaying a provocative exterior.

The tension remained, however, and at some point in the ensuing months it culminated in a suicide attempt. Whether it was genuinely intended or not, Meyer was diverted from blowing his brains out – another way to *épater le bourgeois* perhaps? – by the fortuitous appearance of a publisher's flyer under his door at the very moment he was raising the pistol. He picked it up, and found an advertisement for a new book 'On life after death'. This dramatically serendipitous event was sufficient to stir an interest in the occult, and for several years after this he was seriously involved, becoming for instance a founder-member of the Theosophical Society branch in Prague (1891). Such activity is perhaps reflected in a passage from *What's the use of White Dog Shit?* where the narrator remarks in passing that 'the next thing I did was to immerse myself in the study of the history of secret socie-ties. There can't be a single fraternity left that I haven't joined . . .'

Meyrink is clearly not incapable of self-irony, for he did indeed join a number of similar organizations, becoming for instance (in 1893) an 'Arch Censor in the Mandala of the Lord of the Perfect Circle'. Again perhaps this provides an oblique clue to the all-seeing qualities ascribed to the perfect sphere in *The Truth-drop*. He read deeply in the literature of the occult, taking an interest especially in its Indian and Tibetan connections. *The Violet Death*, *The*

Opal and *The Black Ball* each illustrate the mysterious power that he felt underlay such esoteric knowledge. He did however rapidly become disillusioned with the institutions of the occult, even while retaining a belief that enlightenment comes to the individual only through the individual effort of the brain, and he persisted in a belief in the curative powers of yoga, which he practised for many years. Its residual impact on the stories is however ambivalent, and overlaps with the influence of hallucinogenic drugs, with which he also experimented at this time.

Meyrink is for instance fond of representing figures in yoga-like poses and trances: 'I took up the pose, raised both arms above my head in imitation of the statue, and lowered my fingers until the nails just brushed my scalp ... ... I cannot believe that I could have fallen asleep. Suddenly there seemed to come echoing out from somewhere inside me a sound ...' (*Dr. Cinderella's Plants*). In this passage it becomes uncertain whether what then follows is an account of a real experience or just a mad vision. Similar behaviour, directed towards some kind of control of the events surrounding the protagonist, can be found for instance in *The Ring of Saturn*, or in *The Man on the Bottle*, where there is also a parallel set of contortions/distortions, this time affecting the victim of a cruel punishment.

Alternatively, other stories should rather be read as visions of a drug-fevered mind: *Bal Macabre* for instance offers the consequences of a bout of mushroom poisoning, while *Fever* or *Rupert's Drops* suggest the more familiar atmosphere of an opium-induced dream. *A Suggestion* goes further, towards Gogol's *Diary of a Madman* perhaps, or even Maupassant's story of spectral obsession *Le Horla*, in recounting the stages by which a mind gradually collapses into insanity.

Slightly more conventional science also plays a role in these tales, though it too can be treated with a satirical eye. Meyrink makes fun of popular naiveté in describing the panic induced by an image of a chameleon appearing in the night sky (*Dr. Lederer*), but on a less surreal level he touches, sometimes quite uncannily, on ideas well ahead of his time. The villain of *Petroleum, Petroleum* who threatens to suffocate the world by covering the entire surface of the oceans in oil is undoubtedly more believable (and consequently terrifying) now than he was in 1902. *The Truthdrop* offers an insight into the universe mirrored in a single droplet of liquid: it does not take too much imagination to see a parallel in the invention of television. And *The Black Ball* presents to the reader familiar with modern cosmological theory a genuinely frightening scenario more real than anything Meyrink could have supposed, in portraying the mystic powers of oriental thought which, allied to the emptiness of certain Western minds, can produce a black hole that can swallow up an entire universe.

He is however not averse occasionally to turning the tables, by demonstrating the superiority of scientific theory to experience, as for instance in *The Automobile*, where we are treated to a demonstration of why the internal combustion engine cannot possibly work: a theory spectacularly and explosively proved in the denouement of the tale, though there is also something uncanny about the accuracy of the professor's prediction – or is it just his supreme mathematical ability?

In yet other tales Meyrink offers a more light-hearted and whimsical touch. *The Curse of the Toad – curse of the toad* with its curious motif of repetition resurrects a very simple, and very old, joke dressed up in mysterious eastern splendour; *The Secret of Hathaway Castle* has all the trappings of gothic horror to disguise the problem faced by anyone charged with the expense of maintaining a large and decaying property. Similarly, *G.M.* also presents an elaborate joke, though this one does have the hard edge of satire directed at planning authorities and human greed. The motif of the lure of buried wealth here is a topic which recurs in such stories as *Chimera* or *Coagulum*, though the latter also hints at something much more unpleasant than gold that is hidden, as does, *a fortiori*, the tale of *The Urn of St. Gingolph*. Buried in another sense, within one's

9

own head, the secret of *Humming in the Ears* reveals a common acoustic phenomenon in psychologically disturbing terms.

The interest in oriental occultism when allied to a particular aspect of medical science gives rise to some of the most vividly disturbing of all Meyrink's stories, in which the malign and mysterious figure of Dr Mohammed Daryashkoh repeatedly reappears. *The Brain*, *Dr Cinderella's Plants*, *The Waxworks* and *The Preparation* are all morbidly obsessed with the scientific possibilities inherent in anatomical deconstruction, and the horrific preservation of the vital functions of mere parts of humans. Meyrink is fascinated by the opportunities presented by a post-*Frankenstein* world, and the darker aspects of medical practice are thus revealed.

On a more down-to-earth level, he can flirt with eroticism (*Bal Macabre*, *Izzi Pizzi*, *Blamol*) to uncover a seamier side of the world that 'respectable' society prefers not to acknowledge, and he does not miss any opportunity to attack the smug, browbeating and blinkered complacency of established doctrines, especially within the medical profession, as for instance *The Brain* reveals, where the eminent medical Professor ignores the most dramatic event of the tale which leads to the death of Martin Schleiden, because he is so anxious to stress the failure of the victim to follow his instructions. Schleiden has just died of shock at seeing a brain spill out from a plaster head dropped by a man carrying it in the street. Meyrink's implied suggestion is that the brain is somehow mysteriously connected with Schleiden's own displaced consciousness, in consequence of a disagreeable experience he had at the hands of some witch-doctors in the Sudan. But all the professor can say, brushing such ideas aside – or rather, not contemplating them at all – is that 'you are asking me about irrelevancies which I have neither the time nor the leisure to pursue . . . I have in the most explicit terms prescribed to your brother a total abstention from any kind of excitement. This was a Medical Prescription! Your brother was the one who chose not to follow that advice.' A similar attitude is taken in *The ardent Soldier* where in the face of an 80 degree fever the possible involvement of an Indian medicament as the cause is dismissed as 'irrelevant', and a nonsensical explanation in pseudo-medical jargon is offered, which is supposed to pacify the curiosity of the ignorant public.

The particular quality of bile reserved for doctors in these stories, matched only by Meyrink's hatred of the military, and especially of its officer corps, can in part be accounted for by reference to further episodes in the life of this, in the view of the upright citizenry of Prague, highly unorthodox banker.

In 1900 he suffered a kind of paralytic trauma, identified by his doctors as tuberculosis of the spine. Conventional treatment having little effect (*The Invalid* perhaps reminds us of this experience), Meyrink was convinced that his yogic exercises were more beneficial than any medication, and came to believe in due course that they had indeed cured the condition. It is not surprising then to find that the sea-lily in *Blamol* similarly suffers paralysis on eating a 'Blamol' pill, and that the pompous cuttlefish doctor should assert, without a trace of irony, that 'Blamol works, like all such agents, not when you take it, but only when you spit it out.' The title of the story is, incidentally, almost certainly a pun on 'Darmol', a popular patent digestive remedy of the time.

Meyrink's high-profile and eccentric behaviour, his illegitimate origin and an irregular liaison with the woman who was to become his second wife (in 1905) while his first wife (whom he married in 1893) refused to divorce him, all contributed towards a latent conflict with a bourgeois society expecting a different set of principles from a banker, and this culminated in 1901 in Meyrink learning that while he had been ill, he had been gravely insulted by an Army Reserve officer (and a medical man to boot) Dr Hermann Bauer. Meyrink demanded satisfaction in a duel. This was refused, on the grounds of his known illegitimacy. To have accepted his challenge, and thus to treat him as an

11

equal, honourable and worthy opponent would apparently have damaged Dr Bauer's military honour. The ending of *Coagulum* amply illustrates Meyrink's feelings on that score.

Others took advantage of his weak position at this time too, accusing him of irregular banking practices. The outcome of it all was a period of imprisonment from January to April 1902 (an experience of which the story *Terror* is perhaps a reflection) while the case was investigated, only to be dropped when the principal witness vanished on realising that his accusation was about to be shown to be worthless. The damage was however by then done: as a banker Meyrink was ruined, and he was obliged to turn elsewhere. The *Simplicissimus* satires over the next seven years were the result.

The impact of these stories was immense. They certainly contributed to an increase of some 500% in the circulation of *Simplicissimus* over the period in which they appeared. But they were strong meat for some, and with the advent of the First World War their open satire, especially of military ideas, attitudes and competence, and their depiction of the officer class in particular as empty-headed strutting peacocks (*The Black Ball*) driven by blind nationalism (*Wetherglobin*) became unacceptable to established representatives of authority.

In 1916 the collected volume of 52 stories in all was banned in Austria, and especially after (and perhaps because of) the huge increase in his popularity following the publication of *The Golem* in 1915, which put him among the most famous of living German authors, Meyrink became more and more the focus for nationalist attacks, which used him as a scapegoat for the lack of progress in the War, impugned his patriotism, accused him of ungentlemanliness and lacking in decent manners (The *Ring of Saturn* was pilloried as an insult to German womanhood), and drew attention to his supposed Jewishness – his actress mother Maria Meyer being wilfully or otherwise confused with a Jewish actress Clara Meyer. One critic (Bartels) remarked sarcastically that Meyrink might well deny being a Jew, but his literary character and style were still typical of one. The very success of *The Golem*, albeit short-lived, which was at least partly to be ascribed to nothing more than astute publicity and advertising, but whose content also chimed in with the mood of 1917, a prevalent desire to escape from the present horror into a perceived fictional occult horror, contributed to his vilification as unpatriotic and decadent. It is notable that Meyrink's *Collected Works* of 1917 in fact omit five of the stories that had appeared in the edition of 1913.

The attacks on Meyrink were fundamentally directed at the satirist, but by now he had moved on, withdrawing from the public eye and concentrating more and more on the esoteric and the occult. He died in 1932, but by then he was a nearly forgotten figure. The Third Reich would of course have no time for him, and it is only in a more recent and sympathetic age that his work has begun to resurface.

THE ARDENT SOLDIER

It had been no small task for the army doctors to treat all the wounded Foreign Legionaries. The Annamites had poor weapons, and the gun pellets almost always stayed lodged in the soldiers' bodies.

Medical science had recently made great strides – a fact known even to those who could neither read nor write, who willingly submitted to all sorts of operations, especially since they had no other choice.

Most of them died, to be sure, but only after their operation, and even then only because the Annamite ammunition had clearly not been sterilised before it was fired, or because it had picked up dangerous bacteria on its flight through the air.

Professor Mostschädel's reports left us in no doubt about that. He had attached himself to the Legion (with official permission) for scientific reasons, and it was thanks to his vigorous measures that the soldiers as well as the natives in the village were now constrained to speak of the magical cures of the pious Indian holy man Mukhopadaya in nothing louder than a whisper.

A final casualty who was brought to the field hospital by two Annamite women long after the skirmish was over was Private Wenzel Zavadil, a Bohemian by birth. When asked where they came from, that they were so late arriving, they explained that they had found Zavadil lying unconscious outside Mukhopadaya's hut, and had then tried to resuscitate him by administering some opalescent liquid which was the only thing they could find in the fakir's abandoned residence.

The doctor could find no injury, and his questioning of the patient only produced a wild growl which he took to be the sound of some Slav dialect. As a cure-all he prescribed a clyster, and strode off to the Officers Mess.

Doctors and Officers got on well together. The short

but bloody skirmish had brought a bit of life to the usual tedium.

Mostschädel had just said a few kind words about Professor Charcot (in order not to emphasis too painfully his superiority, as a German, over his French colleagues), when the Indian Red Cross nurse appeared in the entrance to the tent and reported in her broken French: 'Sergeant Henry Serpollet dead, Trumpeter Wenzel Zavadil 41.2° fever.' 'Intriguing people, these Slavs,' murmured the M.O. 'The fellow has a fever, and yet no wounds!'

The nurse was given an order to stop the soldier's mouth (the one who was still alive, of course) with three grammes of quinine.

Professor Mostschädel had caught the last few words, and used them as the starting-point for a lengthy disquisition in which he celebrated the triumphs of science, which had succeeded in discovering this fine substance quinine in the hands of the ignorant, who had, like a blind chicken, come across the remedy in nature.

He had moved on from this theme to talk about spastic spinal paralysis, and the eyes of his listeners were beginning to glaze over when the nurse reappeared to report:

'Trumpeter Wenzel Zavadil 49 degrees of fever – permission to request a longer thermometer . . .'

'By that reckoning long since dead,' smiled the Professor.

The staff surgeon slowly stood up, and with a severe gesture strode over to the nurse, who took a step backwards. 'You see, gentlemen,' he said observing this, 'the woman is hysterical, just like the soldier Zavadil; a double case!'

And they all relaxed again.

'The Medical Officer requests your presence at once,' rasped the adjutant, waking the academic (who was still very much asleep) as the first rays of the sun lit up the edge of the nearby hills.

Everyone turned to look expectantly at the Professor, who at once made his way to Zavadil's bed.

'54 degrees Réaumur blood-heat. Unbelievable,' groaned the doctor.

Mostschädel smiled in disbelief, but pulled his hand away in astonishment when he actually felt himself burning as he touched the invalid's forehead.

'Give me the history;' he eventually said to the Medical Officer with some hesitation, and after a long and embarrassing silence.

'Give me the history, and don't loiter about so aimlessly!' roared the M.O. at the youngest doctor present.

'Bhagavan Sri Mukhopadaya might know . . .' the Indian nurse dared to begin.

'Speak when you are spoken to!' interrupted the Medical Officer.

'Always the same old superstition,' he went on, turning to Mostschädel.

'The layman always thinks of the inessentials,' agreed the Professor soothingly. 'Send me the report, I have urgent matters to attend to now.'

'Now, my young friend, what have you established?' asked the great expert of the young subaltern, who was followed into the room by a crowd of curious officers and doctors.

'The temperature has reached 80 degrees now . . .'

The Professor waved his hand impatiently. 'And?'

'Patient survived Typhus ten years ago, mild diphtheria twelve years ago. Father died of a fractured skull, mother of concussion; Grandfather skull fracture, grandmother concussion! – The patient and his family come from Bohemia,' explained the subaltern. 'Condition, apart from the temperature, normal. Abdominal functions all sluggish. Wounds, apart from slight contusions to back of head, not apparent. Patient is said to have been treated with an opalescent liquid in the hut of the fakir . . .'

'Stick to the point, young friend. No irrelevancies,' warned the professor good-naturedly, as with a gesture of invitation he indicated the various bamboo chairs and baskets standing in the room to his guests for them to seat themselves. He continued:

'This, gentlemen, as I recognised at once early this morning, but only hinted at to you, so that you might yourselves have the opportunity to find your way to the correct diagnosis, is a not altogether common case of spontaneous thermo-incrementation in consequence of trauma to the calorific node (here his expression facing the officers and the civilians, took on a quality of slight disdain) – of that centre in the brain that controls variations in the temperature of the body – on the basis of inherited and acquired factors. If, further, we consider the subject's cranial structure . . .'

At this point the speaker was interrupted by the repeated notes of a horn advertising the arrival of the local fire brigade (consisting of a few invalid soldiers and Chinese coolies) and presaging horror in the direction of the Mission Building.

Everyone rushed outside, the colonel leading the way.

Trumpeter Wenzel Zavadil was running down the hill from the hospital towards the Lake dedicated to the goddess Parvati. Followed by a shrieking and gesticulating crowd and clothed in blazing rags, he bore a strong resemblance to a human torch.

The poor fellow was met just in front of the Mission by the Chinese fire-brigade in command of a stout jet of water, which admittedly knocked him to the ground, but which almost immediately evaporated in a cloud of steam. – The trumpeter's temperature had at last risen so far as to begin to carbonise all the objects around him in the hospital, and the nurses were eventually obliged to chase him out of the building with iron staves. The floors and stairs showed evidence of his burning tread, as if the very devil had passed by.

And now, the last rags having been torn away by the water-jet, Zavadil lay naked in the courtyard in front of the Mission, steaming like a smoothing-iron and ashamed of his nakedness. From the balcony above a Jesuit father of some resourcefulness threw down an old asbestos suit which had once been the property of a worker in the lava fields, and Zavadil gratefully put it on.

*

'But how in Heaven do you explain how the fellow isn't just a heap of ashes?' the Colonel asked Professor Most-schädel.

'I have always admired your strategic talents, Colonel,' replied the scholar indignantly, 'but as far as medical science is concerned, you must leave matters to us doctors. We must adhere to the facts as they are given to us, and there is for us here no contra-indication that we should ignore them.'

The doctors were highly pleased at this lucid diagnosis, and subsequent evenings were spent in the Captain's tent, where there was always a jovial atmosphere.

Only the Annamites spoke of Wenzel Zavadil any more. From time to time he might be seen on the other side of the lake sitting near the stone temple of the goddesss Parvati, the buttons on his asbestos suit glowing red.

The priests of the temple were rumoured to roast their chickens at his fire; others were of the opinion that he was already cooling down, and was intending to go home to his own country, just as soon as his temperature had got down to 50 degrees.

THE BRAIN

The vicar had been looking forward so much to the return of his brother from southern climes, yet when at last he arrived an hour earlier than expected, and walked into the familiar old parlour at home, all his joy vanished.

What the reason for this might have been he had no idea; he just felt it, as you would feel a November day when the whole world seems to be about to collapse into ashes.

Even the old housekeeper Ursula was lost for words.

Martin was as sunburned as an Egyptian, and smiled affably as he shook hands.

He would certainly stay for dinner, he said, and was not at all tired. He would have to go up to town for a few days, that was true, but then he would be able to spend the whole summer at home.

They talked of their younger days, when their father was still alive: and the vicar saw how the oddly melancholy cast of Martin's features became more pronounced.

'Don't you think that certain kinds of startling or decisive events become just bound to happen precisely because the fear of their happening can't be suppressed?' These were Martin's final words before going to bed: 'And can you remember my awful terror as a child when I once saw a bleeding calf's head in the kitchen . . .?'

The vicar couldn't sleep: it was as if his room, where the atmosphere was usually so pleasant and comfortable, was filled with some kind of eerie, suffocating fog.

'It's only because there's something new here, something unfamiliar,' he thought.

But it wasn't the new or the unfamiliar – it was something else his brother had brought with him.

The furniture had taken on a different aspect from usual, and the old pictures looked as if an invisible force was pinning them to the walls. A nervous foreboding permeated the air, as if merely thinking an outlandish or mysterious thought might precipitate a sudden and unpremeditated change. Just don't think of anything new - stick with the old and comfortably familiar, comes the warning from inside. Thoughts are as dangerous as a bolt of lightning!

The vicar found it impossible to get Martin's adventure after the battle of Omdurman out of his mind: how he had fallen into the hands of the obi-men, who had tied him to a tree . . . then he sees the witch-doctor who comes out of his hut, kneels in front of him, and places a human brain, still covered in blood, on a drum held in front of him by a female slave.

Then he takes a long needle and stabs it into the brain in various places, and each time Martin cries out in pain, because he can feel the pricking inside his own head.

What does it all mean?

The Lord have mercy on him!

On that occasion Martin had been rescued by English soldiers, who brought him back to the field hospital in a state of total paralysis.

One day the vicar found his brother lying unconscious at home.

The butcher had just arrived with his meat-grinder, reported old Ursula, and Mr Martin had inexplicably passed out.

'This can't go on: you will have to go to Professor Diocletian Crammer's Nervous Clinic – he has a world reputation,' the vicar had said when his brother regained consciousness. Martin agreed.

'Mr Schleiden? Your brother, the vicar, has already told me something about you. Please take a seat and tell me briefly what the problem is,' said Professor Crammer, welcoming him to the consulting room.

Martin sat down, and began: 'Three months after the affair at Omdurman – as you know – the last signs of paralysis—'

'Show me your tongue,' interrupted the Professor – 'Hm: no abnormality; slight tremor. Go on then?'

'The last signs of paralysis —' Martin repeated.

'Cross your legs. Good. More. Good' ordered the specialist, producing a little steel hammer, and tapping the patient smartly just below the kneecap. The leg jerked upwards.

'Heightened reflexes,' said the Professor. 'Have you always had heightened reflexes?'

'I don't know,' Martin apologised. 'I've never hit myself on the knee.'

'Shut this eye. Now the other one. Open the left ... yes, now the right – good. Light reflexes normal. Has the light reflex always been normal, Mr Schleiden, especially recently?'

Martin gave up and stayed silent.

'You really should have taken notice of these signs,' remarked the Professor a little reproachfully, and then ordered his patient to get undressed.

A long and exhaustive examination now took place, during which the doctor displayed every sign of deep ratiocination, accompanied by the expression of Latin words *sotto voce*.

'You said earlier something about symptoms of paralysis. I cannot find any,' he said suddenly.

'No, I meant to say that they had disappeared after three months,' Martin Schleiden replied.

'You have been ill for so long, Sir?'

Martin looked nonplussed.

'It is a remarkable phenomenon that almost all German patients are incapable of expressing themselves clearly,' opined the Professor, smiling kindly. 'You should go to a French clinic one of these days. How succinctly even the simple man can express himself. There is not much to say about your malady, by the way. Neurasthenia, that is all. I am sure that even you will be interested to learn that we doctors have succeeded, especially recently, in getting to the bottom of these nervous problems. Yes, that is the blessing of our modern investigative methods, that we can know quite precisely when it is appropriate to use no physical means – such as medicines. Keep the whole syndrome emphatically in view! Day by day! You would be surprised at what we can achieve by these methods. You understand me? And then the important thing is, to avoid all excitement – that is poison to you. And make an appointment to see me every other day. Remember: *No Excitement!*'

The Professor shook the invalid by the hand. He seemed visibly exhausted by his intellectual effort.

The sanatorium was a massive building on the corner of a neat street bisecting the quietest part of town.

On the opposite side there extended the old palace of Countess Zahradka, curtains hanging permanently across the windows reinforcing the morbidly quiet impression conveyed by the empty street.

Almost nobody went past, for the entrance to the busy clinic was on the other side facing the park, by the two old chestnut trees.

Martin Schleiden liked the solitude, and the garden with its carpets of flowers, its bath-chairs and its capricious invalids. He did not like the boring fountains and the stupid ornamental glass balls.

He was drawn to the quiet street and the old palace with its barred and gloomy windows. What might the place look like inside?

Old, faded tapestries, worn furniture, muffled chandeliers; an ancient dame with bushy white eyebrows and hard, austere features, who had forgotten both life and death.

Day after day Martin Schleiden walked past the walls of the old building.

In such desolate streets you have to keep close in to the walls.

He had the characteristic easy stride of a man who has lived long in the tropics. He did not disturb the impression of the street at all: they fitted neatly together, these two unworldly existences.

Three hot days arrived, and on each one of them, in the course of his solitary walk, he encountered an old man carrying a plaster bust. A plaster bust with an ordinary, quite unremarkable physiognomy.

On the third occasion they walked straight into one another – the old man was so clumsy.

The plaster figure slipped out of his grasp and fell slowly to the ground – everything falls in slow motion: it is only those people who have no time to stand back and watch things who are unaware of that fact.

As it struck the ground the plaster split open, and a human brain, all bloody, spilled out.

Martin Schleiden stared at it with a glazed expression, stiffened and went pale. He spread his arms and then buried his face in his hands, before collapsing with a sigh on to the pavement.

Quite by chance the Professor and his two assistants had witnessed everything from a window, and now the victim lay unconscious in the examining room, totally immobile. Half an hour later death supervened.

A telegram had brought the man of the cloth hurrying to the sanatorium, and now here he stood in tears before the man of science.

'How did it all happen so suddenly, Professor?'

'It was to be predicted, my dear Vicar,' replied the great man. 'We adhered strictly to the methods of treatment we doctors have developed over many years of experience, but if the patient himself does not follow what is prescribed for him then all our medical skills are bound to be applied in vain.'

'But who was the man carrying the plaster bust?' broke in the vicar.

'There you are asking me about irrelevancies which I have neither the time nor the leisure to pursue. Allow me to continue. Here in this very room I have in the most

24

explicit terms prescribed to your brother a total abstention from any kind of excitement . This was a Medical Prescription! Your brother was the one who chose not to follow that advice. It pains me a great deal to say so, my dear friend, but you will agree that strict compliance with medical advice is and remains the principal necessity.

I myself was a witness to this unfortunate event: the man claps his hands to his head in a state of great excitement, falters, staggers and collapses to the ground. Of course assistance naturally came too late. I can already predict what the autopsy will establish: Cerebral Hyperanaemia in consequence of diffuse sclerosis of the cerebral cortex.

Now, calm yourself, my dear fellow, and take the proverb to heart: those who make their beds must perforce lie in them.

It sounds hard, but you know, the truth is a cruel taskmaster.'

IZZI PIZZI

My last port of call on a holiday tour of the sights was the 'Goldenes Dachl' in Innsbruck.

Since then I have sworn an oath by Vishnu never to do the same thing again.

I prefer to admit quite publicly that I am depraved. I take no interest in the sort of things that fill the rest of the nation with pride; I am bored by the most revered canons, my heart does not beat one whit the faster at the sight of Clothilde the Chaste's lacy breast-binders.

A fellow like me knows of nothing better than to wander about the streets when he's on holiday, watching people go by, standing for hours in the flea-market or gazing into shop windows.

I had spent another day in just this fashion, and when evening came I fetched out my compass and set out in a direction that would take me most quickly and assuredly away from the city theatre.

A policeman had assured me on his honour that there wasn't another one, so I was quite easy in my mind.

Not long after, I was reading the boldly captioned poster advertising the 'Vienna Orpheus Society' by the light of a red lantern suspended above it.

'Izzi Pizzi, the charming young songstress, the 'Pride of Hernals' makes her debut again today' I read. I put a hand to my breast pocket to check that I still had my wallet secure, and with the bold stride of a seasoned rake I stepped through the portal of the 'Black Horse' as the place was called – evidently named after its bearded proprietor who directed me towards a glass door.

I entered a long, narrow room, packed with people, and sat down at the table marked 'reserved' – to those in the know a sure indication that rakes are permitted to sit there. Izzi Pizzi is just about to take the stage with her lovely ballad 'Down at Larkey Meadow where we met the soldier boys'. And every time she comes to 'Larkey' she produces an inimitably graceful wave of the arm, and steps back with her left foot on its elegant point.

She, or no-one, whispers my thumping heart.

I call to the waiter, pull out a silver florin and invite the beauty to supper. It's half-past eleven, and the performance will soon be at an end.

Etelka Horvath, a dark Hungarian lass, slim as a riding crop, stamps her way to the concluding bars of a marvellously intricate Czardas, accompanying herself with a stream of 'oi's and 'ai's.

'The lady will be with you presently.'

I put on my hat, abandoning my coat where it is, and go across the yard to the '*chambre séparée*'.

The table has been laid.

– But for *three* people? Aha – it's that stupid trick with the chaperone.

And then all those glasses? By heaven, what can be done about it? I fall into deep thought.

An idea that might save me: 'Waiter, send across to Franz Maader, wine merchant in the Eisengasse, for a big stone jar of Ochishchenya. Got it? Ochishchenya, O-chish-chen-ya.'

There's a sound at the door. A strawberry-coloured cloak trimmed with a row of undulating blonde feathers and surmounted by a blue hat like a millstone comes in. I take three steps towards this apparition and offer a grave and dignified bow.

The cloak is first to introduce itself: 'Izzi Pizzi.'

'Baron Semper Saltomortale, from the foothills of Mount Athos,' I reply with majestic self-possession.

Two big blue eyes observe me mistrustfully. I offer the lady my arm, and lead her to the table.

But what have we here? A shapeless lump of black silk with enamel buttons has already found its way to a chair. I stare more closely. The devil! Have I gone mad? Or was the old hag hidden in the piano all the time?

I help the young beauty into a chair.

He really is a foreigner, she thinks.

'My governess,' she introduces the old woman. 'I hope you don't mind.'

The waiter reappears: I rush across and pin him against the door. 'Look here, I'm not paying any fancy bills, or yesterday's tabs. And mind you give us the almonds without their shells, and no phillipines at all either.'

The waiter winks conspiratorially with his right eye, and I press a tip into his hand, of a quality that only reigning dukes can usually expect.

'And hang my stick there, too,' I add aloud, to discourage the ladies from harbouring any suspicions.

Izzi Pizzi orders for herself 'Caviare for starters – a whole tinful, so's we don't have to keep ringing.'

'Caviare is very healthy,' she turns to *me* with an ardent glance.

'In my country every gentleman always carries a lemon,' I add, with a knowing air.

'Sorry, caviare's gone: will sardines in oil be alright?' says the waiter.

Izzi Pizzi flares up. 'But there was a whole big tinful outside!' 'Just lead shot, Miss' replies the brave fellow, remembering the size of his *douceur*. 'Alright then. Crabs – a dozen of them!'

'Izzi is an unusual Christian name,' I say to her, when she has at last finished ordering. 'That's just my stage name. Actually I'm called Dinah. 'There's nobody finer than your little Dinah'.'

'Witty, like all Viennese, my dear.'

'That's what the Count always says, don't he, Izzi?' interjects the old woman with a simper.

'The Count who is always so jealous?' I ask.

'You know already . . .?'

'Counts are always jealous,' is my reply.

I'm treating the little ballad-singer like a grande dame, conjuring up the most abstruse and exotic manners.

Beads of perspiration bedeck the old woman's brow – brought on by all her compulsive smiling.

Izzi feigns suppressed passion, adding in her mind a retaliatory zero to the figure she imagines represents the contents of my wallet.

'Multiply it by five,' I say, out of the blue.

She jumps with a start. 'How did you know? What made you say that?'

Can he read thoughts? she wonders.

Her guardian gives me a glassy stare, wondering if I've gone mad. I'm thinking of some evasive answer when the waiter comes in with the crabs.

The two 'ladies' watch perplexed, waiting to see what strange ritual I'm going to perform. I let them wait, in the meanwhile polishing my monocle with great care.

The old woman coughs and pulls at her enamelled skullcap. The young one fiddles with her blouse.

At last I take pity on them, look sorrowfully at my fingernails, pick up a crab and wrap it in my serviette before putting it down again on the table.

Izzi has already copied me: the other one is rather more cautious. Then with my fist I come down hard on the bundle, open it up and pick out the shattered remains.

The old woman gapes in astonishment. 'You'll never get the stains out of the washing,' she blurts out.

'Shh,' whispers the other, giving her a kick under the table.

Inside me all the joy of hell breaks loose.

'The Rhenish was acid, and the Burgundian over the top,' said little Dinah, relieved that the stupid meal was over, and with it the opportunity to make herself look silly.

The old crone had just picked at everything.

You see, you old bag, I think to myself, if you were a student of mythology, you'd know what the immortal Tantalus had to suffer!

But now we come to the Champagne, you poor, star-struck fool, she thinks, giving me a better-disposed look: anyone can drink how he likes, there's no funny stuff there.

'Just put a bottle of Pommery to cool, à l'américain, waiter. Then we'll move on to another sort. In the meanwhile you can uncork the stone jar there and bring two medium sized water glasses, one for the lady there! I won't presume to offer it to you, my dear Miss,' I say, turning towards Izzi. 'It heats up the blood a little.'

'What's in it, then?' she asks inquisitively.

'Ochishchenya – table wine, a Russian thirst-quencher, which we always drink before Champagne, both ladies and gentlemen. It looks just like ordinary water, as you can see.' And I pour out a full glass for the old woman. Mine I fill with genuine water, without anyone noticing.

'You have to swallow the whole glassful at one go, otherwise the taste is spoiled; permit me to show you how, madam – thus . . .' I have no idea what Ochishchenya is made of. I don't even know if its inventor was a real human being. I only know that fumic nitric acid is warm christening water by comparison.

I was overcome by a feeling of compassion as I saw the old woman really swallow the full glass down as instructed.

Even Chingachgook, the great Mohican chieftain would have fallen dead.

But the chaperone twitched not a muscle: she looked down and put a hand up to her coiffure.

Now, I think, she is going to pull out a long hatpin to thrust into my heart. But nothing of the kind. 'Really excellent, Herr Baron,' she says, looking me straight in the eye.

'Let me have a taste,' lisps Izzi, taking a little sip.

And she fishes out an insect that has fallen into the glass and trills, oh so knowingly: 'these flies look like Spanish flies, Spanish flies, Spanish flies.'

I'm not going to drop my role though, and I retain my conventional demeanour.

When Izzi's knee brushes against mine, I say 'pardon' and look across apologetically at the 'governess'. The girl eventually loses patience and sends the old woman to bed. I thrust the stone jar into her arms as she leaves, and wish her a truly quiet night.

So, now we shall get all the well-rehearsed old stories one after the other about her deprived childhood and so on; all about how she gave herself to some gentleman merely to pay off her brother's gambling debts.

The old woman who has just left is a relic of the days when she was just a tomboy scampering round the estates of her aristocratic father: a faithful old retainer. And how she hates the count who watches her so jealously! All she is short of is a few florins in cash to pay some small debts, boot-repairs and suchlike, which she is too proud to admit to him, and she would give him the brush-off on the spot. And then her colleagues! Oh God, what shameless hussies - better not to speak of them!

I look at Izzi quizzically. It's true, she has assumed a serious expression and fairy-tale eyes.

'Etelka Horvath went on stage for the last time. The public hissed her off,' she begins.

Aha, I say to myself. Variety is the spice of life: she's starting at the end.

'Today she got a room over there in the Bavaria Hotel the ... the Hungarian. I'm here in the house, the Black Horse, up on the first floor. After seven I'm not allowed to go out, nor may I receive visitors in my room. The Count is a miserable tyrant,' she continues. 'And then it's a Police Regulation, too,' I add dreamily.

'That too,' she concedes, embarrassed, 'but from nine in the morning I am at home to visitors - and I stay in bed till twelve!'

Pause. My foot brushes hers.

She leans back, watching me with half-closed eyes; I can hear her teeth chattering as she quickens her breathing.

At once I fetch the feathered cloak from its hook on the wall, and place it round her shoulders. 'You must go to bed, my girl, you're really feverish.'

We walk back across the courtyard to the hotel entrance, and at the porter's lodge at the foot of the stairs she stops to say goodbye. 'Are you going straight home, or back into the Café, Baron?'

'I must get up early tomorrow: I've a call to make at nine,' I reply, looking straight into her eyes. 'I lost my heart this evening – but you'll promise to keep it quiet?'

The girl nods her blue velvet hat uncertainly.

'Then I'll tell you: I'm absolutely gone on sweet Etelka, your charming partner.'

Izzi sweeps away up the stairs; I stay at the bottom, bathed in a glow of satisfaction and whistle a little tune:

> 'For the rose
> And the girl
> Are just asking
> To be plucked.'

THE VIOLET DEATH

The Tibetan stopped talking.

His lean figure stood immobile for some moments, and then disappeared in the jungle.

Sir Roger Thornton stared into the fire. If that fellow hadn't been a Sanyasin – a holy man – that Tibetan, who was furthermore on a pilgrimage to Benares, he would, of course, not have believed him. But a Sanyasin neither lies, nor can he be deceived. And yet, what was to be made of that horrible and treacherous-looking facial twitch he had?

Or had the firelight deceived him, reflected as it was so oddly in those Mongolian eyes?

Tibetans hate the European, and jealously guard their magic secrets, with whose aid they hope one day to destroy all foreigners, when the time is right.

Be that as it may, he, Sir Hannibal Roger Thornton is determined to see with his own eyes whether these remarkable people do really have occult powers in their possession. But he is in need of companions, bold men, whose determination will not falter even when the terrors of another world lurk behind them.

And the Englishman surveys his companions in his mind. Among the Asians only the Afghan over there comes into the reckoning: fearless as a beast of prey, yet superstitious. Otherwise, there is only his own man – a European.

Sir Roger prods him with his stick. Pompeius Jaburek has been totally deaf since the age of ten, but he knows how to lip-read every word.

Sir Roger Thornton explains to him, with elaborate gestures, what he has learned from the Tibetan. Some twenty days march from here, in a distant, but precisely identified Himalayan valley, there is a quite remarkable district. Surrounded on three sides by sheer cliffs, its only access is barred by a belt of poisonous gas which bubbles up continuously out of the ground and which instantaneously kills any animal that attempts to pass across it. The canyon itself, extending over about fifty square miles, is said to be the home of a small tribe of Tibetan origin, who live in the middle of the luxuriant forest, wear pointed red caps and worship some devilish creature in the shape of a peacock. In the course of centuries this satanic beast has taught them the black arts and has revealed to them secrets that will revolutionise the world, teaching them a certain kind of chant that can in an instant destroy the strongest of men. Pompeius smiles in scornful disbelief.

Sir Roger explains that he proposes to overcome the poison belt with the aid of diving helmets and back-packs loaded with compressed air, and so explore the secret of the valley beyond.

Pompeius Jaburek nods in agreement, and rubs his dirty hands gleefully.

The Tibetan had not lied. There below lay the mysterious gorge, filled with the most magnificent verdure, but bordered by a yellowish-brown belt of loose, eroded desert earth about half an hour's march wide, and cutting the valley off completely from the outside world.

The gas escaping from the ground was pure carbon monoxide.

Sir Roger Thornton, having surveyed the distance to be crossed from a hilltop vantage point, decided to make a start the very next day. The diving helmets which he had had sent from Bombay were functioning perfectly.

Pompeius shouldered both repeating rifles and a variety of instruments that his master had deemed indispensable. The Afghan had stubbornly refused to join them, declaring that he was always ready to enter a tiger's lair, but would consider very carefully before doing anything that might endanger his immortal soul. So the two Europeans remained as the only ones bold enough.

The copper diving helmets glinted in the sunlight and cast fantastic shadows across the spongy ground from which the poisonous gas rose in countless tiny bubbles. Sir

Roger had struck out at a bold pace to ensure that the compressed air would suffice to make the crossing of the gas belt. Everything looked hazy, as if seen through a thin wall of water. The sunlight was a ghostly green colour, tinting the distant glaciers – the gigantic profile of the 'roof of the world' – and giving them the appearance of a grotesque desert.

And now they had already reached a patch of fresh grass, and lit a match to confirm the existence of atmospheric air at every level above the ground.

Then they both took off their helmets and packs. Behind them the wall of gas shimmered like a mass of water. The air was filled with the scent of Amberia. Glittering butterflies, as big as a hand and strangely decorated, spread their wings on the motionless flowers like the pages of a book of magic incantations.

Walking some distance apart the two explorers made their way towards a patch of woodland that obscured the view beyond.

Sir Roger gave his deaf assistant a sign – he seemed to have heard a noise – and Pompeius cocked his rifle.

They passed round the edge of the wood and came upon an open meadow. Barely a quarter of a mile away a group of about a hundred men, evidently Tibetans and wearing red pointed caps, were standing in a semicircle: they were already expecting the intruders.

Sir Roger strode fearlessly towards them, with Pompeius some yards to one side.

The Tibetans were dressed in traditional sheepskins, but looked for all that hardly like real people; their expressions were so frighteningly ugly and their features so unnatural, with an aspect of terrifying and superhuman evil. They allowed the explorers to get quite close, when suddenly, at the command of their leader, they shot their hands in the air and clapped them over their ears, at the same time giving voice with all the power of their lungs.

Pompeius Jaburek looked quizzically across at his master, and raised his rifle, for this strange concerted movement in the crowd seemed to signal an attack: but what he now saw froze his blood.

A shimmering, whirling cloud of gas had formed around his master, similar to the one they had just passed through. The figure of Sir Roger seemed to be growing shapeless, as if it were being worn away by the swirling gas. The head tapered to a point and the whole mass dissolved in a heap: where before the lean Englishman had been there now stood nothing but a bright violet-coloured cone, about the size and shape of a sugar-loaf.

The deaf Pompeius was seized with a wild fury. The Tibetans were still shouting, and he gazed fixedly at their lips, trying to read what it was they were shouting.

It was the same word, over and over again. Then suddenly their chief stepped out from among them, and they stopped, at the same time uncovering their ears and letting their hands fall. Like panthers they leaped upon Pompeius, who responded with a volley from his rifle, stopping them in their tracks for a moment. Instinctively he shouted back at them the word he had just read on their lips:-

'Emelen – Emmel-len' he roared until the cliffs echoed again.

A kind of dizziness overtook him, he saw everything as if through a pair of pebble-spectacles, and the ground turned beneath him. It lasted only a moment and then his vision cleared again.

The Tibetans had vanished, as his master had before them, and he was faced instead by an army of violet sugar loaves.

The chief was still alive. His legs had already sunk into a bluish porridge and his body was beginning to subside, as if the whole man was being digested by some completely transparent entity. He was wearing, not a red cap, but a structure resembling a Mithraic building, in which living yellow eyes could be seen moving about.

Jaburek brought the butt of his gun down on his skull, but couldn't avoid the sickle-shaped knife the dying man flung at him as he fell, which struck his foot.

He looked all round. There was not a living thing in sight. The scent of the Amberia had increased and become almost pungently suffocating. It seemed to emanate from the violet cones that Pompeius was now examining. They were all identical, consisting of the same gelatinous and slimy material. It was quite impossible to sort out the remains of Sir Roger Thornton from amongst all these coloured pyramids.

With a gnashing of teeth Pompeius kicked aside the Tibetan's face and hurried back the way he had come. In the distance he could see the copper helmets glinting in the grass. He pumped up his diving gear and stepped into the gas belt. The crossing felt as if it would go on for ever, and the tears rolled down the poor fellow's face. Oh God, oh God, his employer was dead; dead, here in the depths of India! The ice-giants of the Himalayas yawned at the sky – what did they care for the sorrows of one puny human heart?

Pompeius Jaburek faithfully wrote down everything that had happened, word for word, just as he had experienced and seen it, though he still could not understand, and sent it to his master's secretary in Bombay, 17 Adheritollah Street. The Afghan undertook delivery. And then Pompeius died, for the Tibetan's sickle had been poisoned.

'There is no god but Allah, and Mohammed is his Prophet,' intoned the Afghan, bowing his forehead to the ground. The Hindu hunters had strewn the corpse with flowers, and burned it on a pyre, chanting their own songs of piety.

Ali Murrad Bey, the secretary, turned pale at the frightful news, and passed the letter on to the editors of the *Indian Gazette*.

And the modern Deluge began.

The *Indian Gazette*, containing *The Case of Sir Roger Thornton* came out a good three hours later than usual next day. A strange and horrifying incident was the cause of the delay:

Mr. Birendranath Naorojee, managing editor, and two assistants, who were in the habit of checking through the

37

paper every day at midnight before publication, had vanished from the locked office without trace. In their place three bluish-coloured jellylike piles were found on the floor, with the newspaper proofs lying between them. The police, with their usual stolid pomposity had scarcely put the finishing touches to their first reports before countless similar cases started to be notified. Gesticulating newspaper readers vanished by the dozen under the gaze of crowds surging in panic through the streets. Innumerable small violet pyramids materialised on steps, in market places and in narrow lanes, wherever you cared to look.

Before dusk fell half the population of Bombay had disappeared. An official health decree ordered the immediate closing of the port and interdiction of all commerce with the outside world, as a means of restricting the spread of this novel epidemic (for such it must be) to the greatest extent possible. Telegraph and cable lines hummed day and night, transmitting the frightful news and the account of the case of Sir Roger verbatim across the ocean to the world beyond.

The following day, the quarantine was lifted, as it was already recognised as being too late.

From across the globe came horrific reports that the 'violet death' had broken out everywhere almost simultaneously, and was threatening literally to depopulate the world. Everywhere reason was sacrificed, and the civilised world resembled nothing so much as a vast anthill, stirred up by the smoke of a peasant boy's pipe.

In Germany the plague first appeared in Hamburg. Austria remained inviolate for some weeks, since they only read local newspapers.

The first case to appear in Hamburg was particularly tragic. Pastor Stuhlken, whose venerable age had made him somewhat deaf, was sitting early one morning at the breakfast table in the bosom of his large family. Theobald, his eldest son, puffing at his long student pipe, his dear wife Jetta, daughters Nina, Tina — in short everyone was there, the whole family. The old man had just opened the

38

English paper that had just arrived, and was reading aloud the item reporting the case of Sir Roger Thornton. He had just read past the word 'Emelen', and was reaching for his coffee-cup when he realised with horror that he was surrounded by a group of mucilaginous cones. One of them still had the tobacco pipe projecting from it.

All fourteen souls had been taken up unto the Lord. The pious old man collapsed in a dead faint.

One week later more than half the human race was dead.

A German scholar was entrusted with the task of casting at least some light on these events. The fact that it was the deaf, and deaf-mutes who seemed immune gave him the idea (which was quite correct) that the epidemic was due to a purely acoustic phenomenon.

In the seclusion of his study he composed a long scientific paper, which he announced as a public lecture in a few key phrases.

His discussion consisted more or less in drawing attention to a number of almost totally forgotten Indian religious texts concerning the creation of fluid astral vortices by means of reciting certain secret words and formulae, and in supporting these descriptions by reference to the most recent discoveries in the fields of vibration and radiation theory.

His lecture was held in Berlin and, on account of the enormous interest it evinced, his orotund sentences had to be relayed by megaphone to the assembled public.

This memorable address closed with the lapidary words: 'Go to your ear-specialist, who will remove your hearing, and take care never to say aloud the word 'Emelen'.'

One second later, the scholar and his entire audience were nothing more than blobs of slime, but the manuscript remained, in time gained currency and credence, so that humanity was at least prevented from dying out altogether.

A few decades later, in the 1950's, a new deaf and dumb generation has inherited the earth.

Habits and customs have changed, rank and material

wealth displaced. An ear-surgeon rules the world, music has been consigned to the alchemical formulae of the Middle Ages. Mozart, Beethoven and Wagner are objects of derision, as were, in their time, Albertus Magnus and Bombastus Paracelsus.

In museum torture-chambers the occasional dust-covered piano bares its old keys.

Author's Postscript: The reader is advised **not** to pronounce the word 'Emelen' aloud.

TERROR

There is the sound of jangling keys and a platoon of prisoners marches out into the prison yard. It is noon, and they must walk round on a circular track two by two, one behind another, to breathe the open air.

The courtyard is paved. Only in the middle are there a few patches of dark grass, like the mark of graves. There are four spindly trees and a pathetic looking privet hedge.

All round rises a line of old, yellow walls pierced by small, barred cell windows.

The prisoners in their grey penitentiary clothing say little as they walk on, round and round, one behind the other. Almost all of them are sick. Scurvy, swollen limbs; faces as grey as putty, eyes blank. With cheerless hearts they plod on at the same pace.

The warder with sword and cap stands at the door, staring in front of him.

A strip of bare earth runs round by the walls. Nothing will grow there: misery trickles through the yellowed stones.

'Lukavsky's been to see the governor,' a prisoner calls down in an undertone from his window to the men below. The troop treads on. 'What's up with him?' asks a new arrival of his neighbour.

'Lukavsky, the murderer, he's been condemned to hang, and today's the day they're deciding whether to confirm it. The governor's been reading him the sentence in his office. Lukavsky said nothing – just staggered a bit –but outside he was gnashing his teeth and working up a rage. The screws have put a straitjacket on him and strapped him to the bench so's he can't move till the morning, and they've put a crucifix in front of him.' Bit by bit all this is called out to the marchers as they go by, by the man inside.

'He's in No. 25, that Lukavsky,' says one of the old lags. They all look up at the bars on the window of No. 25.

The warder leans idly against the door and kicks away an old piece of bread lying on the path.

In the narrow corridors of the old district courthouse the cell-doors stand together in close rows: low oaken doors set into the solid walls and armoured with iron bands and massive locks and bolts. Every door has a barred opening barely a handspan square. It is through this that the news has crept, whence it flutters along the bars from mouth to mouth: 'He'll hang tomorrow!'

It's all quiet in the corridors and throughout the whole building, and yet there is everywhere a faint noise. Slight, inaudible, only to be felt. It presses through the walls and dances in the air, like a cloud of midges. Life : bound, incarcerated life!

In the middle of the main entrance, at a point where it widens out, an antique, empty chest stands in the dark.

Slowly, silently the lid rises, and a shudder of mortal fear sweeps into every corner of the house. Words die on the prisoners' lips as it goes by, and there is not a sound in all the corridors, only the beating of one's own heart and a rushing in the ears.

The trees and bushes in the yard are motionless, their autumnal branches grasping paralysed at the murky air. They seem to have grown suddenly darker.

The group of prisoners comes to a stop as if by a command. Was there not a cry?

From the old chest a hideous worm slowly begins to emerge, a gigantic leech. Dark yellow in colour, with black flecks, it sucks its way along the floor, past each cell in turn. Alternately growing fat and then elongating it gropes its way along, searching. On each side of its head a cavity encloses five close-packed lidless and immobile eyeballs. This is terror.

It slithers along until it finds a condemned man, and then fastens on to him, below the throat, just where the great artery runs bringing life up from the heart to the head, and there it sucks the vital blood, enveloping the warm body in its slippery coils.

And now it has reached the murderer's cell.

There is a long, horrible shriek, a shriek without end, a single tone that reaches into the courtyard.

The watcher leaning on the doorpost jumps back to life and pulls open the gate. 'Back to the cells, you men, march!' he shouts, and the prisoners go past him and up the steps without looking at him, tramp, tramp, tramp in their clumsy hobnailed boots.

Silence again. The wind whips down into the deserted yard, tearing off an old skylight that rattles and crashes down in splinters on to the dirty earth.

The condemned man is able to move nothing but his head. In front of him the whitewashed wall of the dungeon. Impenetrable. Tomorrow at seven they're coming to get him. Eighteen hours to go. And seven before it's night. It'll soon be Winter and then Spring will come, and hot Summer. And he'll get up early, at dawn, and walk aong the street, looking at the old milk-cart, with the dog harnessed in front. Freedom! He can dó what he wants.

And then his throat tightens again; if only he could move – damn, damn, damn – and beat his fists on the walls. To get out! To break everything, bite through the straps. He doesn't want to die now, no, he doesn't! They could have hanged him *then*, just when he had killed him, that old man; he already had one foot in the grave. He wouldn't have done it now though! His defence lawyer didn't mention that. Why hadn't he called out to his accomplices? They would have judged him differently if he'd done that. He must say so now to the governor. The warder must take him along to see him. Now. Straight away. Tomorrow morning will be too late. The governor will have his uniform on, and you can't get so close to him then. And the governor wouldn't listen to him. It's too late then, you can't send away all the policemen any more. The governor won't do it.

The hangman places the noose over his head. He's got brown eyes, and keeps looking straight at the man's mouth. They heave on the rope, everything starts to turn – stop, stop, he's still got something to say, something important.

Will the warder come today and untie him from the bench? He can't lie there like this for a whole eighteen hours. Of course not – the confessor has still got to come, he's always read that. That's the law. He's not a believer, but he's going to demand a priest, that's his right.

And then he'll smash that arrogant parson over the head with the stone jug there . . .

His tongue's as dry as dust. He wants a drink, he's thirsty. Oh Lord, oh God, why don't they give him anything to drink? He'll make a complaint, when the inspector comes next week. He'll drown him in it, the screw, the bloody pig. He'll scream until they come and untie him, louder and louder, until the walls fall down. And then he'll be out in the open air at last, high up, so they won't find him when they come looking.

He must have fallen somewhere, he thinks. He felt such a jerk just now.

Has he been asleep? The light is dim.

He tries to put a hand up to his head: his hands are tied fast. From the old tower the time drones out, one, two – how late is it then? – six o'clock. Oh God in Heaven, only thirteen more hours and they'll wrench the breath from his body. He's going to be executed, hanged, with no mercy. His teeth start chattering with the cold. Something is sucking right at his heart, he can't see. Then everything goes black. He screams, but he can hear no scream; everything about him screams, his arms, his chest, his legs, his whole body, all the time without ceasing, without pausing for breath.

An old man with a white beard and a hard, forbidding face steps towards the open window of the office, the only one without bars, and looks down into the yard. The screaming irritates him, he frowns, murmurs something to himself, and slams the window shut. The clouds scud across the sky in long, curling lines. Tattered hieroglyphs, like old, half erased writing: '*Judge not, that ye be not judged!*'

PETROLEUM, PETROLEUM

In order to secure to myself the priority of
prophecy, I must point out that this story
was written in 1903.

Gustav Meyrink

On Friday, at midday, Dr. Kunibald Jessegrim poured the
strychnine solution gently into the stream.

A fish rose to the surface, dead, floating belly upwards.

You'd be as dead as that, by now, said Jessegrim to
himself, and stretched, glad that he had emptied away his
suicidal thoughts along with the poison.

Three times in his life he had looked Death in the eye in
this way, and each time he had been locked back into life
by a vague premonition that there was still some great
deed, one wild, grand act of revenge waiting for him.

The first time he had wanted to put an end to it all was when
his invention had been stolen, and then again ten years later,
when he had been hounded out of his job because he had never
given up pursuing the thief in order to expose him, and now,
because – because – Kunibald Jessegrim groaned aloud as
thoughts of his overwhelming misery welled up once more.

Everything had gone, everything he had depended on,
everything that had once been dear to him.

And it was that blind, narrow-minded, baseless hatred of
the crowd, driven by slogans to oppose everything that did
not conform to dull mediocrity, that had done this to him.

To think of all the things he had undertaken, had
thought of and suggested!

He had scarcely got going before he had to stop in the
face of a 'Chinese wall' – the generality of obstinate humanity, and the cry of 'but . . .'

'The Scourge of God' – yes, that's the solution, Dear
God Almighty make me a destroyer, an Attila! and the
fury blazed up in Jessegrim's heart.

Tamburlaine, Genghis-Khan limping across Asia, and devastating the fields of Europe with his Golden Mongol Horde, the Vandal Kings, who found peace only on the ruins of Roman art – all these were of his kind, powerful brothers in barbarism, born in the same eagle's nest.

A monstrous, limitless affection for these creatures of Shiva grew in him. He felt that their dead spirits would stand by him, and another type of existence flashed into his body.

If he had been able to look into a mirror at that moment these miracles of transfiguration would no longer have presented a mystery.

Thus it is that the dark powers of nature surge into our blood, profoundly, and of a sudden.

Dr. Jessegrim was possessed of extensive knowledge. He was a chemist, and he found it easy enough to succeed.

In America such people get on well. It is no surprise that he was soon making money – a lot of money.

He had established himself in Tampico in Mexico, and made millions out of a lively trade in mescal, a new anaesthetic and social drug, whose preparation he had developed.

He owned four square miles of estates around Tampico, and the huge reserves of oil beneath them promised to multiply his wealth beyond measure.

But that was not the object for which his heart yearned.

The new year was approaching.

'Tomorrow is January 1st 1951, and those lazy creoles will have yet another reason for spending three days on the binge and dancing their fandangos,' thought Dr. Jessegrim, looking down from his balcony at the tranquil ocean below.

'And it'll be hardly any better in Europe. The papers will be coming out in Austria about now – twice as fat as usual, and four times as stupid. A picture of the new year as a naked boy; a new calendar full of women in diaphanous clothes and holding cornucopias; notable statistics: on Tuesday at 35 minutes and 16 seconds past 11 it will be exactly

9 thousand million seconds since the inventor of double entry bookkeeping went to his eternal (and well-deserved) rest – and so on.'

Dr. Jessegrim sat and went on staring at the glassy sea, shimmering so strangely in the starlight, until midnight struck.

Midnight!

He took out his watch and wound it slowly, until his fingertips felt the resistance of the winder. He pressed gently against it, and then more strongly ... there, a slight click and the spring was broken. The watch stopped.

Dr. Jessegrim laughed a mocking laugh. 'That's how I shall twist your springs too, you ...'

A frightful explosion rocked the town. It echoed from far away in the south; the old seafarers reckoned its source would be found somewhere near the great peninsula between Tampico and Vera Cruz.

Nobody had seen any signs of fire, nor was there any indication from the lighthouses.

Thunder? At this season? And under a clear sky? Impossible. Probably an earthquake therefore.

Everyone made the sign of the cross. Only the landlords of the shebeens fell to cursing, for all their customers had deserted the bars, and had run to the hills behind the town where they told each other fantastic tales of their escape.

Dr. Jessegrim took no notice: he went into his study humming a little tune: farewell, my land of Tyrol ...

He was in a superb frame of mind as he fetched a map from the drawer and pricked it off with a pair of dividers, referring to his notebook and taking pleasure in the way everything fell into place. As far as Omaha, possibly even further to the north the oil-fields stretched, there couldn't be any dispute about that any more, and he knew now that underground the oil must be present in great lakes, bigger even than Hudson's Bay.

He *knew* it: he had worked it out, he had spent twelve whole years on the calculations.

According to his view the whole of Mexico lay across a series of caverns under the earth, which in large measure, at least in so far as they were full of petroleum, were all interconnected. His life's work had been gradually to blast away any remaining dividing walls. For years he had employed armies of men at the work: what a mint of money that had cost!

All those millions he had made in the mescal business had gone into it.

And if just once he had struck oil it would all have been in vain. The government would have stopped him blasting – they didn't like it anyway.

Tonight was the night when the last walls were to go: those against the sea, on the peninsula, and further north near St. Louis Potosi. The explosion would be automatically controlled.

Dr. Kunibald Jessegrim pocketed his few remaining thousand dollar bills, and drove off to the station. The express to New York left at four in the morning.

What else was there left to do in Mexico?

He was right: there it was in all the papers – the verbatim telegram from along the Mexican Gulf coast, abbreviated according to the international cable code:

'EXPLOSION CALFBRAIN BERRYMUSH' which approximately translates as 'Seasurface completely covered in oil; cause unknown, everything stinks. State governor.'

This interested the Yankees enormously, as the occurrence was without a doubt bound to make a great impression on the stock exchange and to push up the value of petroleum shares. And property dealing is the best part of life, after all!

The bankers of Wall Street, when questioned by the government about whether the event would cause a rise or a fall in the exchange shrugged their shoulders and declined to make a prediction before the cause of the phenomenon should be discovered; and in any case, if the market reacted contrary to reason there would undoubtedly be a great deal of money to be made.

The news made no particular impression on European sentiment. In the first place they were covered by protective tariffs, and in the second place they were in the process of bringing in new laws, which involved the planned introduction of voluntary triennial numeric enforcement, together with the abolition of men's proper names, which was intended to stimulate patriotism and encourage a better attitude towards military service.

Meanwhile the oil was busily spewing out of the subterranean Mexican Basin into the sea, just as Dr. Jessegrim had predicted, forming an opalescent layer on the surface that spread further and further, and which, carried by the Gulf Stream, soon seemed to cover the entire ocean.

The shores were devastated and populations withdrew inland. What a shame about those flourishing cities!

And the sea took on a fearfully beautiful quality: a smooth surface, extending into infinity, glinting and shimmering in all sorts of colours, red, green and violet, and then again a deep, deep black, like images from a fantastic starscape.

The oil was thicker than petroleum customarily is, and in its contact with the salt water seemed to undergo no other change than that it slowly lost its smell.

The expert opinion was that a precise investigation of the causes of this phenomenon would be of great scientific value, and since Dr. Jessegrim's reputation (at least as a specialist in Mexican petroleum reserves) was well established, they lost no time in seeking his opinion as well.

This was brief and to the point, even if it did not deal with its subject in quite the expected way.

'If the oil continues to flow at the present rate, the entire oceanic surface of the planet will, by my estimation, be covered in 27–29 weeks, leading to a total cessation of rainfall in the future, since there will no longer be any opportunity for evaporation. In the best case it will only rain petroleum.'

This frivolous forecast aroused violent disapprobation and yet it appeared with every succeeding day to gain in probability, and as the invisible springs showed no sign of drying up, but on the contrary seemed to be augmenting in quite extraordinary fashion, a panic terror began to overcome the whole of humanity.

Every hour brought new reports from the observatories of Europe and America – even the Prague Observatory, which had so far contented itself with taking photographs of the moon, gradually began to focus on these new and extraordinary phenomena.

In the Old World nobody was talking about the new military proposal any longer, and the author of the draft law, Major Dressel Ritter von Glubinger ab Zinkski auf Trottelgrün sank into oblivion.

As always in confused times, when the signs of disaster stand ominously in the sky, the voices of discontent, who are never satisfied with the status quo, could be heard as they dared to question hallowed institutions.

'Down with the army, wasting our money! Waste, waste waste! Build machines, think of ways to save mankind in its desperate plight from the threat of petroleum!'

'But that won't do' warned the more circumspect. 'You can't simply put so many millions of people out of a job!'

'What do you mean, out of a job? The troops only need to be paid off. Everyone of them has learned something, even if it's only the most elementary trade,' came the reply.

'Oh yes, that's all very well for the men – but what are we to do with the officers?'

Now that was a significant argument.

For a long time opinions swayed back and forth, with no party gaining the upper hand, until the encoded message came via cable from New York: 'HEDGEHOG POUNDWISE PERITONITIS AMERICA', meaning: 'Oil flow increasing, situation extremely dangerous. Wire by return whether the smell is as bad with you. Regards. America.'

That was the last straw.

A popular demagogue, a wild fanatic rose up, mighty as a rock against the breakers, hypnotic, spurring the people on to the most ill-considered actions by his oratory.

'Away with these games! Let the soldiers go, and make the officers useful for once. Give them new uniforms if it makes them feel better – bright green with red spots, if it's my choice. Send them down to the beaches with blotting paper to mop up the oil, while the rest of us think of a way out of this frightful mess.'

The crowds shouted assent.

The counter-suggestion that such measures could hardly have any effect, and that it would be better to use chemical means found no favour.

'We know, we know all that,' came the reply. 'But what are we going to do with all those redundant officers, eh?'

THE CURSE OF THE TOAD –
CURSE OF THE TOAD

Broad, moderately agitated, sedate
The Mastersingers

On the road to the Blue Pagoda the Indian Sun beats down – sun beats down. People are singing in the temple, strewing white blossoms before Buddha, while the priests chant: Om mani padme hum; om mani padme hum. The streets are empty and deserted: today is a holiday.

The tall stems of cusha-grass had formed a guard of honour along the meadows beside the road to the Blue Pagoda – the road to the blue pagoda. The flowers waited on the millipede, who lived across the way under the bark of the venerable old fig tree.

The fig tree was the most exclusive residential district.

'I am the Venerable,' he said of himself, 'and from my leaves Swimming Trunks can be made - swimming trunks can be made.'

But the great toad, who always sat on the stone, despised him for being an old stick-in-the-mud, and she had no interest in swimming trunks. She hated the millipede too. He was inedible, for he was too hard, and was full of Poisonous Juice – poisonous juice.

For that reason she Hated Him – hated him.

She wanted to destroy and ruin him, and had spent all night in communion with the spirits of toads long deceased.

And now she had been sitting on the stone since sunrise, waiting and twitching her hind leg from Time to Time – twitching her hind leg from time to time.

Now and then she spat at the cusha-grass.

All was silent: blossoms, beetles, flowers and grass, and the broad, broad sky. It was a holiday.

Only the old batrachians in the pond croaked out their profane songs:

> 'To hell with lotus blossoms
> To hell with life,
> To hell with life . . .'

There came a gleam from under the bark of the fig tree, and a string of black pearls shivered shimmering down, curled languorously and, raising its head, danced playfully in the glittering sun.

The Millipede – the millipede.

The fig tree rubbed his leaves in delight, and the cusha-grass Rustled Ecstatically – rustled ecstatically.

The millipede scuttled across to the big stone, where his dance-floor lay: a bright, Sandy Patch – sandy patch.

And he swept about in curls and swirls until, bedazzled, all his spectators were compelled to Close their Eyes – close their eyes.

The toad gave a sign, and from behind the stone her eldest son stepped forward. With a profound obeisance he proffered a written communication from his mother to the millipede.

With foot No. 37 the latter accepted it, and enquired of the cusha-grass if it was all properly stamped and franked.

'We are the oldest grass in the world, we know, but that we don't know. The laws change every year. Indra Alone knows that – Indra alone knows that.'

The spectacled cobra was sent for, who read the letter aloud, as follows:

'*To the Right Honorable Gentleman, Mr. Millipede.*

I am but a poor, wet, slippery thing, despised of the earth, whose spawn is considered beneath both plants and animals. I do not shine, I do not glitter. I have but four legs – but four legs, not a thousand like you – not a thousand like you, oh most honorable! Blessing upon you, Nemescar, Nemescar!'

'Nemescar, Nemescar,' chimed in the wild roses of Shiva, repeating the Persian Greeting – the Persian greeting.

'Yet wisdom resides in my head, and deep knowledge – deep knowledge. I know the grasses, all of them, by name, I know the number of the stars in the sky, and of the leaves of the figtree, the stick in the mud. And my mind has not its equal among all the toads of India.

But lo, even so I can count things only if they stand still, and not when they are in movement – not when they are in movement.

Tell me then, oh most honourable one, how it can be that when you walk you always know which foot to begin with: which is the second, and the third, which one comes next as fourth, fifth, sixth – whether the next is the tenth or the hundredth; what meanwhile the second is doing, and the seventh: is it standing, or moving; when you get to the 917th, whether you should lift the 700th, put down the 39th, bend the 1000th or stretch the fourth – stretch the fourth?

I pray you, tell me, poor wet slippery thing, who has but four legs – but four legs, and not one thousand like you – not one thousand like you: how do you do it, O most Honourable One?

Respectfully,
Toad'

'Nemescar,' whispered a little rose-blossom, who had almost fallen asleep. And the Cusha-grass, the flowers, the beetles and the figtree, and also the spectacled cobra gazed expectantly at the millipede. Even the Croakers were silent – croakers were silent.

But the millipede was glued to the ground, paralysed, unable to move one single joint.

He had forgotten which leg to lift first, and the more he thought about it, the less he could Work It Out – work it out.

And along the road to the Blue Pagoda, the Indian Sun burned down – the Indian sun burned down.

THE BLACK BALL

Originally it was just a kind of fable, a rumour spreading out quite generally from its source in Asia to the centres of Western culture. It was said that in Sikkim, south of the Himalayas, the Gosains, as they are called, an order of uneducated, almost barbarian holy men, had come up with a truly fabulous invention.

The Anglo-Indian papers carried the story, though they seemed less well informed than the Russians; those who know the ways of the place were not surprised, as it's well-known that the Sikkimese make a point of treating everything English with detestation.

This was probably the reason why news of the mysterious invention reached Europe via Petersburg and Berlin.

The academic world was thrown into turmoil when the phenomena were demonstrated.

The great lecture hall, dedicated otherwise to purely scientific presentations, was packed.

On a podium in the middle stood the two Indian experimentalists: the Gosain Deb Shumsha Jung, his gaunt features liberally smeared with white, sanctified ashes, and the dark-skinned Brahman Rajendralalamitra, wearing the insignia of his caste, a slender cotton ribbon hanging down from his left shoulder.

A number of glass vessels had been suspended on wires from the ceiling, so that they hung at eye-level; traces of white powder were visible inside them. An unstable explosive, probably iodide, as the interpreter suggested.

The Auditorium fell silent as the Gosain went to one of the flasks, wrapped a narrow gold chain around its neck and attached the two ends either side of the Brahman's forehead.

He then stepped round behind him, raised both arms into the air and began to recite the mantra – the incantatory formula – of his sect.

These two ascetic figures were standing absolutely still, with that peculiar form of immobility singularly characteristic of aryan Asiatics when they are sunk in religious meditation.

The Brahman's black eyes were focused on the flask. The onlookers held their breath.

Many of them were obliged to close their eyes, or to look away, in order to avoid a fainting fit. The sight of such petrified figures has an hypnotic effect, and people started to ask their neighbours in an undertone if they too didn't think that the Brahman's face sometimes looked as if it were wreathed in mist.

This impression was, however, merely caused by the sight of the holy tilak-sign on the Indian's dark skin: a large white U, worn by every believer as a symbol of Vishnu the Saviour, on forehead, chest and on each arm.

Suddenly a spark inside the flask ignited the powder. There was a momentary puff of smoke, and then as it cleared there appeared inside the flask — an Indian landscape of indescribable beauty. The Brahman had projected his thoughts into the glass!

It was the Taj Mahal at Agra, that magic palace of the Great Mogul Aurungzebe, in which he had, centuries ago, imprisoned his father. The bluish white cupola of snow-like crystal, together with the slender minarets at its sides, of a magnificence that would force you to your knees, could be seen eternally reflected in the perpetually shimmering water bordered by dream-drenched cypresses.

An image that reawakens a secret longing for forgotten fields, swallowed up in the deep slumber of one's wandering soul.

There was a buzz of voices in the audience; amazement and curiosity as the flask was detached from its support and passed from hand to hand.

Such a fixed, three-dimensional thought-picture (said the interpreter) would survive for months, inasmuch as it had sprung from the vast and consistent imaginative power of Rajendralamitra. Projections by European brains, in contrast, would have nowhere near such colour or longevity.

Numerous similar demonstrations now took place, in the course of which sometimes the Brahman again, sometimes one or other illustrious academic fixed the gold chain to his forehead.

It was in fact only the images projected by the mathematicians that were at all clear. By contrast, the results excogitated by heads of a juridical capacity were most peculiar. General amazement and a universal shaking of heads, however, greeted the concentrated effort of that famous practitioner of Internal Medicine, Professor Mauldrescher. Even the solemn Asiatics were amazed: an incredible jumble of small, discoloured lumps appeared in the glass, followed by a mass of blurry blobs and points.

'Like an Italian salad,' said one theologian derisively – but he had carefully ensured that he had not been drawn into the experiments. Especially near the middle, where in the case of scientific thought conceptions of physics and chemistry condense (as the interpreter stressed), the material seemed to be totally pickled.

Explanations of why and by what means the phenomena were actually produced were not forthcoming from the Indians. 'Later perhaps, later,' they said in broken phrases.

Two days later another demonstration took place, this time on a more popular level, and in another European metropolis. Once more the same breathless hush among the public, followed by the same exclamations of amazement, as an image of the strange Tibetan fortress of Taklakot took shape under the imaginative influence of the Brahman.

Once more the same more or less meaningless fancies engendered by the city worthies.

The medical men smiled in embarrassed fashion, but were not this time to be persuaded to think into the flask.

When at last a group of military officers stepped forward everyone drew respectfully aside – well, of course they would!

'Gustl, whatd'ye say, why don't ye think of somethin!?' remarked one brilliantined lieutenant to another.

'Not me, far too civvy for me, don't you know.'

'Come, gentlemen, come, someone here shall volunteer' asserted the Major testily.

A Captain spoke up: 'You there, interpreter, is one permitted to think of something imaginary? I wish to think of something imaginary.'

'What shall it be then, sir?' ('Let's see what that peacock can do!' shouted someone from the crowd.)

'No, no, I was just going to think of the military code of honour.'

'Oh,' and the interpreter stroked his chin. 'Hm – I think, I do think, sir, that the flasks are perhaps not strong enough.'

A First Lieutenant pushed his way forward. 'In that case, allow me.'

'Yes, yes, leave it to Kashmacek,' the chorus went up, 'He's a sharp fellow.'

The First Lieutenant put the chain to his head.

'Excuse me, sir,' the interpreter (in a state of some embarrassment) offered him a cloth: 'excuse me, sir, but pomade is rather an insulator.'

Deb Shumsha Jung, the Gosain in red loincloth and chalky face positioned himself behind the officer. He looked even more uncanny here than he had done in Berlin.

Then he raised his arms.

Five minutes went by.

Ten minutes. Nothing.

The Indian gritted his teeth with the effort; the sweat was running down into his eyes.

There, at last! The powder hadn't actually exploded, but a velvet-black ball, as big as an apple, appeared floating free inside the glass.

'It'll never work,' said the officer, excusing himself with an embarrassed smile as he stepped down from the stage.

The crowd roared with laughter.

The Brahman caught hold of the flask in amazement; as

he did so the floating ball, disturbed by the movement, came into contact with the side. The glass shattered instantly, and the splinters as if drawn by a magnet flew into the ball and vanished without trace.

The velvet-black object hovered motionless in the air. Actually, the thing looked not so much like a ball: it gave the appearance more of a yawning chasm. And indeed it was nothing other than a *hole*.

It was an absolute: a mathematical 'nothing'. What happened then of course was the inevitable consequence of this 'nothing'. Everything adjacent to it of necessity fell into it, and became on the instant equally 'nothing', that is, it vanished absolutely.

In fact, there began a violent roaring noise, getting louder and louder, as the air in the ball was sucked into this Black Hole. Pieces of paper, gloves, ladies' veils, everything was swallowed up.

When one officer poked at it with his sabre the whole blade disappeared, as if it had melted.

'This is too much,' expostulated the Major. 'I'm not putting up with this. Come, gentlemen, that's enough!'

'What on earth were you thinking of, Kashmacek?' asked his fellow-officers as they stalked out.

'Me? Well – er, only what we usually think of, don't ye know.'

The crowd, unable to explain the phenomenon, and conscious only of the terrifying and ever-increasing roar, pressed more urgently towards the doors.

The only ones who remained were the two Indians.

'The whole universe as it was created by Brahma, sustained by Vishnu and destroyed by Shiva, will in due course sink into this Hole,' said Rajendralalamitra solemnly.

'That is the curse on us, brother, for coming to the West!'

'What does it matter,' murmured the Gosain. 'We must all in time enter into the negative realm of existence.'

THE PREPARATION

The two friends were sitting in a corner of the Radetzky Cafe by the window, deep in conversation.

'He's gone – he went off with his man to Berlin this afternoon. The house is completely empty: I've just been round there to check. Those two Persians were the only inhabitants.'

'So he really did fall for that telegram?'

'I never doubted he would for a moment. The name of Fabio Marini will make him do anything.'

'That surprises me a bit, since he lived with him for so long – until he died, in fact. What else could he expect to find out about him in Berlin?'

'Aha! Professor Marini is supposed to have kept quite a lot secret from him – he said so himself once, in passing, about six months ago, when dear old Axel was still with us.'

'Is there really something in this mysterious preparation method that Fabio Marini invented, then? Do you honestly believe in it, Sinclair?'

'It's not at all a matter of 'believing'. When I was in Florence I saw with my own eyes a child's corpse that had been prepared by Marini. I tell you, anyone would have sworn the child was just asleep – not a trace of rigor, no wrinkles or creases – it even had the pink skin of a living being.'

'Hm . . . You think the Persian may actually have murdered Axel and . . .'

'That's not something I'd swear to, Ottokar, but it is the moral duty of us both to get to the bottom of what happened to Axel. What if some kind of poison had merely produced an analogue of rigor mortis in him? My God, when I think how I pleaded with the doctors at the Institute of Anatomy – begged them even to make some attempt at resuscitation. What on earth are you getting at, they said, the man is dead, that's obvious, and any interference with the body without Dr Daryashkoh's permission is quite improper. And they showed me the contract which explicitly said that after Axel's death his body was to become the property of whoever owned the document, and in respect of which he had already received, on such and such a date the sum, duly receipted, of 500 Crowns.'

'No, really? That's horrible! And to think that something like that is legal in this day and age. The more I think of it the more incensed I get. Poor old Axel! If he had only known that this Persian, his worst enemy, might come to own the contract. He always thought the Institute of Anatomy itself . . .'

'And the lawyer couldn't do anything?'

'It was pointless. They wouldn't even take any notice of the old milkwoman's evidence, who had once seen Daryashkoh in his garden at sunrise cursing Axel's name for so long that he started foaming at the mouth. Of course, if Daryashkoh hadn't qualified as a doctor in Europe . . . But what's the point of talking – are you coming or not, Ottokar? Make up your mind.'

'Sure, I'll come – but take care we don't get caught as burglars! The Persian's got a spotless reputation as a scholar. Mere reliance on suspicion, for Heaven's sake, is hardly a plausible reason. Don't get me wrong, but are you absolutely sure you weren't mistaken in thinking you heard Axel's voice? Don't get angry, Sinclair, please, but tell me again exactly what happened that time: weren't you just a little bit worked up somehow beforehand?'

'But not in the least! Half an hour before that I had been up on the Hradschin, looking at Wenceslas' Chapel and St. Vitus' Cathedral again; you know what old buildings they are, with those sculptures that look as though they're made of congealed blood and which always make such a deep and unaccountable impression on my soul whenever I see them. And then I went to the Hunger Tower and along Alchemists' Lane to the steps down from the Castle, and was brought up short at the little door in the Castle wall that leads to Daryashkoh's house, because it was standing open. And at the very same moment I heard a voice – it must have come from the window, and I'll swear it was Axel's voice – calling out: one – two – three – four.

God, if only I had gone in straight away; but before I could pull myself together from the surprise that Turkish servant of his had slammed the door shut. I tell you, we've got to get into that house! We must! What if Axel were really still alive? Look, nobody will find us; who ever uses those steps at night-time anyway? And you've no idea how good at picking locks I am these days!'

The two friends passed the time wandering idly up and down the streets before embarking on their plan. Then at dusk they scaled the wall and at last found themselves standing before the Persian's antiquated house.

This isolated building stands on the slopes of Fürstenberg Park, leaning like some inanimate watchman against the wall that encloses the grass-grown steps up to the Castle.

'There really is something horribly sinister about this garden and those old elms down there,' whispered Ottokar Dohnal. 'Look how the Hradschin stands out so threateningly against the skyline. And those windows, all lit up in the embrasures of the wall! Even the air is different, here on the Kleinseite, as if all the life in it has drained off deep underground for fear of the Death that stalks above.
Don't you ever get the feeling that this whole shadowy scene will one day just vanish like a mirage, a *fata morgana*, and that all the pent-up life that's waiting here somewhere in suspended animation will suddenly revive, wraithlike, and turn into something totally and horribly unexpected? I know I do. And just look at those gravel paths down there, glimmering white, like veins.'

'Oh, do come on!' urged Sinclair. 'My knees are knocking with all the tension. Here, hold the map for me.'

The door was soon opened and the two of them felt their way up an ancient staircase, which was barely illuminated by the light of an overcast sky striking fitfully through the round windows.

'We'll have no lights, Ottokar – they might be seen from down below, or from the summer-house outside: follow me closely ... watch out, there's a broken tread here. The door to the corridor is open ... here, here on the left.'

They suddenly found themselves in a room.

'For Heaven's sake don't make such a noise!'

'I couldn't help it – the door slammed of its own accord.'

'We shall have to strike a light. I'm afraid of knocking something over all the time, there are so many chairs in the way.'

At that moment a blue spark blazed on the wall, and they heard a sound like a sighing intake of breath. A faint grating noise became apparent, seeming to come from floor and walls, and out of all the joints in the woodwork at once. There was a moment of total silence again, and then a croaking voice started, loud and slow: *One . . . two . . . three.*

Ottokar Dohnal cried out, scraping madly at his matchbox, his hands quivering with fear. At last there came a light - light! And the two friends were revealed staring at each other, chalk-white. 'Axel!' – – – *fo-our . . . fffive . . . sssix . . . ssseven . . .*

The counting was coming from an alcove in the corner.

'Light the candle – quick, quick!'

eight . . . nine . . . te-en . . . ele...

Suspended from a copper rod hanging down inside the recess was a blond-haired human head. The lower end of the rod had been driven straight through the top of the skull, and the neck below the chin was concealed under a silk scarf. Beneath it projected trachea, bronchi and two pink lungs. Between them, beating steadily, was the heart, surrounded by a number of gold-coloured wires which led away to some kind of electrifying machine on the floor. Fat veins, gorged with blood, carried the circulation up from two narrow-necked reservoir bottles.

Ottokar Dohnal had put the candle down on a little stand, and was now clutching his friend's arm in a faint.

It was Axel's head, with carmine lips and a blooming complexion – alive. The eyes, widely staring and with a wild expression were focussed on a burning-glass hanging on the wall opposite and which seemed to be draped with Asiatic weapons and hangings.

Everywhere they could make out the bizarre designs of oriental fabrics.

The room was otherwise filled with preserved animal specimens – snakes and apes in various contorted poses amidst a jumble of books lying about on the floor.

In a large glass bowl on a bench at the side a human abdomen was floating in a bluish liquid. Gazing gravely down upon the whole scene from a pedestal above was the plaster bust of Fabio Marini.

The onlookers stood, struck dumb, staring hypnotised by the heart of this monstrous human clock, beating and quivering with life.

'God help us, let's get away. I'm going to pass out. Damn that Persian monster!'

They made for the door. As they did so there came again that queer grating noise, seeming to come this time directly from the preparation's mouth itself. Two blue sparks flashed, and were reflected by the burning-glass precisely into the pupils of the dead eyes opposite. The lips parted, the tongue poked out and curled behind the front teeth as the voice rasped: a quarr – ter passst.

The mouth closed and the face stared blankly out again.

'Horrible, horrible – the brain is still functioning – it's still alive. – Out, get out, – into the open! The candle, get the candle, Sinclair!'

'Open the door, for God's sake! Why can't you open it?'

'I can't – there, look there!'

The handle on the inside of the door had been replaced by a hand, a human hand, with rings on its fingers – the dead man's hand, in fact. The fingers curled in the air.

'Come on, use a cloth! What are you afraid of? It's only old Axel's hand!'

Outside in the corridor they watched as the door swung slowly shut behind them. A black glass plate on the outside was inscribed:

Dr Mohammed Daryash-Koh
Anatomist

The candle-flame flickered in the draught wafting up the tiled stairwell.

Ottokar staggered to the wall and fell to his knees with a groan: 'Look, look at that!' – He was pointing to the bell-pull. Sinclair held the candle closer, then with a loud exclamation dropped it, and the tin candlestick clattered away down the stone steps. In the darkness they followed it in a mad rush to the bottom, hair standing on end, lungs bursting with the effort.

'Persian Fiend – The Persian Fiend!'

DR. LEDERER

'Did you see that flash? Something must have happened at the power station. Right over there, behind the houses.'

A few people had remained standing, looking in the same direction. A bank of cloud lay heavily over the town, darkly blanketing the valley: a haze, rising from the roofs, unwilling for the stars to make fun of a foolish population.

There was another flash from the slope, lighting up the sky and then vanishing.

'Heaven knows what that is; just now it was on the left, and now it's over there?! Perhaps it's the Prussians' suggested someone. 'What would they be doing here, I ask you. Anyway, I saw the Generals sitting in the Hotel de Saxe not ten minutes ago.'

'Well, *that's* no reason; but the Prussians! That's not even a joke -it couldn't possibly happen even here.'

Suddenly, a dazzling bright oval disc, of huge dimensions, appeared in the sky. The crowd gazed up, open-mouthed.

'A compass, a compass', cried fat Frau Schmiell as she rushed out onto her balcony.

'In the first place, it's called a *comet*, and in the second place it ought to have a tail', said her superior daughter, in a crushing tone. Sounds of amazement broke out all over the town, running through streets and alleyways, in through doors, down dark passages and up narrow stairs until they penetrated the lowliest garrets. Everyone pulled their curtains aside and flung open their casements. A sea of heads peered in an instant from the windows: Ah!

Up in the fog of the night sky a glowing disk, and in the middle of it the silhouette of a great monster, like a dragon.

As big as Josefsplatz, pitch black, with a hideous snout – Just like Josefsplatz.

A chameleon, a chameleon! horrible.

Before the people had pulled themselves together the phantom had vanished, and the sky was as dark as ever.

The crowd went on staring up into the air for hours, till they got nosebleeds – but nothing more appeared.

It was as if the devil had played a joke on them.

'The beast of the apocalypse', was the Catholic opinion, and they crossed themselves, over and over again.

'No, no, a chameleon', rejoined the Protestants, soothingly.

The shrill clang, clang, clang of an ambulance broke through the crowd, who scattered shrieking in all directions as the vehicle came to halt outside the low door of one of the houses.

'Is something amiss here? What is the problem?' enquired the municipal medical officer, ploughing a stately course through the human tangle. They were just bringing a stretcher out of the house, covered with sheets.

'Lord, sir, the fright has brought the Mistress's pains on,' wailed the parlourmaid, 'and it must be eight months at the most – the Master says he knows just exactly when.'

'Frau Cinibulk has come a cropper over the monster,' the word went round. The crowd grew restless.

'Make way, for Heaven's sake, get out of the way, I must get home,' came a few voices.

'Let's go home, we must see to our wives,' mocked some vulgar bystanders: the mob shouted approval.

'Quiet, you rabble,' roared the medical man with a curse – and went off home as fast as possible.

Who knows how long the crowds could have stayed out in the streets if it hadn't started to rain. But gradually the narrow lanes and open squares emptied until nocturnal silence descended on the damp cobbles, shining dully in the light of the lamps.

That night though marked the end of conjugal bliss for the Cinibulks. That a thing like that should happen in such a model marriage! If only the child had died, at least. Eight-month babies usually do, after all.

The husband, Tarquinius Cinibulk (City Councillor) was in a lather of rage. The street urchins followed him whooping down the road. The country nursemaid had an attack of the vapours when she saw the child, and he had to put an advertisement in the paper printed in big letters, requesting a blind replacement.

Then the very next day after this frightful event he had had to use all his persuasive powers to get the representatives of Castan's Panoptikon out of his house, who wanted to see the little monster, and engage it for their next international exhibition.

Perhaps it was one of these people who (in a gesture rather designed to diminish his joy in fatherhood even more) had suggested to him that perhaps his wife had deceived him, for shortly after this he had rushed off to the Police – who were not only not disinclined to accept the odd silver item as a Christmas present but had indeed gained their promotions largely through the assiduous pursuit of characters they deemed suspicious.

So it was barely eight weeks later when the news came out that Councillor Cinibulk had cited a certain Dr. Max Lederer for adultery. The public prosecutor naturally took the case up with the approval of the Police, even though there was no *in flagranti* evidence.

The case took a most interesting turn. The prosecution based its argument on the striking resemblance between the little monster, mewling naked in a pink cradle, and Dr. Max Lederer.

'You will observe, my lords, in particular, the lower jaw and the bandy legs, to say nothing of the low forehead (if one may call it that at all). Note, too, the protruding eyes, and the bigoted and brutish expression on the child's face, and compare the whole with the features of the defendant,' said counsel. 'If then you can have any doubt of his guilt . . .!'

'Nobody will try to deny a certain resemblance,' broke in the defence, 'I must, however, particularly emphasise that this resemblance does not derive from any relationship between father and child; it resides rather in a mutual resemblance to a chameleon. If anyone here is guilty, it is the chameleon, and not the defendant! Bandy legs, my lords, pop-eyes, my lords, even a lower jaw such as that . . .'

'Come to the point, sir!'

Counsel for the defence gave a deferential bow. 'In brief my lord, I would like to call upon expert zoological witnesses.'

After a brief discussion the court dismissed the application with the comment that it had first been decided that expert testimony would be accepted only from those whose profession was the pen. The prosecutor had risen to his feet once more to embark on a new speech, when the defence counsel (who had been deep in consultation with his client) vigorously intervened to draw the court's attention to the child's feet, with the words:

'My lords, I have just observed that the child has on the soles of its feet some of those spots usually described as birthmarks. Could they not have a *paternal*, and not, as is commonly supposed, a *maternal* origin? I beg you most humbly to order an examination: let Herr Cinibulk and Dr. Lederer remove their shoes and socks – and we can perhaps resolve the riddle of paternity in no more than a moment.'

Councillor Cinibulk went very red, declaring that he would rather withdraw his accusation than do anything of the kind. He calmed down only when he was given permission to wash his feet first outside.

The defendant Max Lederer was the first to remove his socks.

As his feet became visible, a roar of laughter echoed round the courtroom, for what was revealed were claws, bifurcated claws indeed, like a chameleon's.

'That's no good: they're not feet at all,' muttered the prosecutor in annoyance, flinging down his pencil.

Defence counsel at once drew the Bench's attention to the fact that it must now be clearly out of the question to suppose that so fine a figure as Frau Cinibulk could possibly have enjoyed intimacy with such an ugly brute. The Court, however, took the view that, after all, the accused would have had no cause to remove his boots in the course of the offence in question.

'Tell me, doctor' said Counsel, turning quietly towards the medical officer, whose good friend he was, under cover of the continuing uproar, 'tell me, couldn't you make a case for mental derangement on the basis of the defendant's pedal deformity?'

'Of course I could – I can do anything: I was a regimental doctor, after all. But we should wait until the city councillor returns.'

But there was no sign of Councillor Cinibulk and he did not return.

The word went round that they would have to wait a long time, and the hearing would have had to be adjourned altogether if the optician Cervenka had not come forward from among the bystanders and given the affair a new twist.

'I can no longer stand aside and see an innocent man suffering: I place myself voluntarily under arrest for disturbing the nocturnal peace. It was I who created that apparition in the sky. Using two spotlights, or 'sun-microscopes' - a marvellous new invention of mine - I projected beams of decomposed, and therefore invisible light into the sky. Where the beams met they became visible, creating that bright disk. The apparent chameleon was simply a small magic-lantern image of Dr. Lederer projected on the clouds, because I had left my own at home. I had, you see, once taken a picture of Dr. Lederer in the sauna, out of curiosity; if Frau Cinibulk caught sight of this image in her heavily expectant condition, it is quite understandable how the child should come to resemble the defendant.'

Then the usher entered, announcing that indeed the soles of the city councillor's feet were beginning to show patches resembling birthmarks, but that the scrubbing would have to continue in case they might yet be washed off.

The court, however, decided not to wait for a result. The defendant was freed for lack of evidence.

THE OPAL

The opal on Miss Hunt's finger excited general admiration.

'I inherited it from my father, who was an old Bengal hand. It used to belong to a Brahman,' she said, stroking the big gleaming stone with her fingertips. 'You only see such fire in Indian jewels - whether it is the way they are cut, or a trick of the light, I don't know, but sometimes the shine has a kind of movement about it, restless, like a living eye.'

'Like a living eye,' repeated Mr Hargrave Jennings thoughtfully.

'Does that remind you of something, Mr Jennings?'

They talked about concerts, balls, the theatre, all sorts of things, but the conversation kept coming back to the Indian opal.

'I could tell you something about these stones – these so-called stones,' Mr Jennings conceded at last, 'but I fear Miss Hunt would find that the pleasure she enjoys in her ring would be spoiled for ever. But if you care to wait a moment, I'll look out the manuscript from my papers.'

The party waited in great suspense.

'Are you ready? What I'm going to read is an extract from my brother's travel notebook – we decided at the time not to publish our experiences.'

So. "Near Mahabalipur the jungle comes down in a narrow strip nearly to the sea. The waterways have been canalized by the government from Madras almost to Trichinopoly, but the Interior is unexplored wilderness, impenetrable and a hotbed of fever.

Our expedition had just arrived, and the dark-skinned Tamil servants were unloading the tents, crates and the rest of the baggage from the boats, in order to have them carried by native porters to the cliff-top town of Mahabali-pur, through the maze of rice-paddies, out of whose rippling sea of green odd groups of Palmyra palms rose like islands.

Colonel Sturt, my brother Hargrave and I immediately took up residence in one of the little temples cut (or rather carved) out of the living rock, which are a true marvel of old Dravidian architecture.

The unexampled work of Indian piety, they must have borne witness to centuries of hymns sung in praise of the great saviour by his inspired devotees – now they serve the Brahman cult of Shiva, along with the seven sacred pagodas with their tall pillared halls hewn out of the rocky ridge above.

Dank mists rose from the plain, hanging over the rice-paddies and meadows, and blurring the rainbow outlines of the homeward-plodding buffaloes harnessed into their rough-built Indian carts. An odd mixture of light and mysterious gloom, that lay heavily on the senses, like a magic haze of jasmine and lilac blossoms lulling the soul into dreams.

Our Mahratta sepoys in their wild and picturesque costumes and red and blue turbans pitched their camp in the ravine below the path up to the rocks, while up above the crash of the waves echoed from the open halls of the pagodas strung out in a line along the coast, like a bellowing sea-hymn in praise of Shiva, the universal destroyer.

As dusk fell behind the hills and the night wind began to blow through the old halls the sound of the waves swelled up to us even louder and more thunderous.

The servants had brought torches to our temple and then gone down again to their people in the village. We set out to explore all the nooks and corners by the flickering light. Numerous dark passageways ran through the rock, and fantastic statues of gods in dancing poses, palms outstretched and with fingers curled in mysterious gestures, cast their shadows across the entrances, guarding the threshold.

How few people they are, who know what mysteries of unimaginable depth, beyond the comprehension of us

Westerners, are signified by these bizarre figures in their sequence and relation to one another, and by the number and height of the pillars and lingams!

Hargrave showed us one such ornament set up on a pedestal, a staff with twenty-four knotted ropes tied along its length, each cord hanging down on either side and divided at the ends: a representation of the human spinal cord. Nearby were images illustrating the ecstasies and transcendental states opened up to the yogi on his path towards miraculous powers, as he fixes his thoughts and feelings on each successive section of the staff.

'This Pingala, great river of Sun,' explained Akhil Rao, our interpreter, in his broken English.

Colonel Sturt caught my arm.'Quiet! – d'you hear that?'

We tensed and listened for a sound in the direction of the passage obscured by a colossal statue of the goddess Kali Bhairab.

The torches crackled – otherwise nothing.

A lowering silence, raising the hair on our necks as our very souls quivered, trembling for that fearful lightning bolt that would stab like an explosion into our lives, and, inescapably, startle all the fatal spectres of the Unknown out of their dark corners and hiding places.

At such moments fear gasps from the rhythmic hammering of one's heart like words, resembling the awful gobblings of the deaf and dumb: *Eugh – gah, eugh – gah, eugh – gah.*

But we strained our ears in vain – everything was silent.

'It sounded like a shriek from the bowels of the earth,' whispered the Colonel.

I had a sense that the great statue of Kali Bhairab, the cholera demon, was on the move. The monster's six arms trembled in the uncertain light of the torches, and her black and white painted eyes rolled like a madwoman's.

'Let's get out into the open, by the entrance,' suggested Hargrave. This is a frightful place.'

*

The town among the rocks lay spread out in the green light like a petrified incantation. The moon shone across the sea in a broad stripe, a huge glowing sword, its point vanishing in the distance. We lay down to rest on the platform. There was no wind, and soft sand had accumulated in quiet corners.

But sleep was hard to find.

The moon rose higher in the sky, and the shadows of the pagodas and the stone elephants shrivelled across the the white rock surface until they were no more than fantastic toad-shapes.

'Before the Moguls came, all these statues are supposed to have been loaded with jewels,' said Colonel Sturt suddenly to me: 'emerald necklaces, eyes made of onyx and opal — .' He spoke quietly, unsure whether I was asleep.

I made no reply.

Suddenly we all started awake in terror. A horrible scream had issued from the temple — a brief howl or a kind of laugh, echoing like metal, or breaking glass.

My brother tore a chunk of blazing wood from its place on the wall and we forced ourselves to go down the passageway into the darkness. There were four of us — what had we to fear?

Hargrave soon threw his torch down, for the corridor opened out into an artificially cut but roofless defile, where the moon cast a harsh illumination, leading us on into a grotto.

The light of a fire was visible behind the pillars. We made our way forward in the shadows.

Flames were rising from a low sacrificial altar, and in their glow a fakir could be seen swaying from side to side, hung about with strings of bones and dressed in the multi-coloured rags of a devotee of Bengali Dhurga.

He was in the middle of reciting an incantation, and in the manner of a dancing dervish was rolling his head rapidly from left to right and then back and forth, his white teeth glinting in the light, and all the time emitting a kind of sobbing whimper.

Two decapitated corpses lay on the ground at his feet: by their clothing we recognised them at once to be the bodies of two of our sepoys. It must have been their death-cries that had echoed so dreadfully up to us.

Colonel Sturt and the dragoman threw themselves on the fakir, but in the same instant he flung them off and they staggered against the wall.

The strength residing in this emaciated ascetic was quite unimaginable, and before we could run to their aid he had already reached the grotto entrance.

We found the severed heads of the two Mahrattas behind the stone."

Mr Hargrave Jennings folded his paper together, adding, 'There's a page missing here, but I can tell you the end of the story. The expression on the faces of the victims was beyond description. My heart still misses a beat when I think of the horror that overcame us all. It would be wrong to call it fear in those fellows' features – it was more like a mad, distorted grin. Their lips and nostrils were drawn up, the mouth wide open, and the eyes – the eyes – it was awful; imagine, the eyes, popping out, showed neither iris nor pupil, but they shone and glistened – just like the stone here on Miss Hunt's ring.

And when we examined them more closely, you could see that they had turned into genuine opals.

A chemical analysis later gave the same result. But how those eyeballs could have changed into opals is still a total mystery to me. I asked a High Brahman about it, and he said it could be done with tantras, and that the process was almost instantaneous, starting from the brain – but who is going to believe that! He added that all Indian opals come from the same source, and that they bring bad luck to anyone who wears them, since they are all exclusively and for ever dedicated to the goddess Dhurga, the destroyer of all organic life.'

The listeners sat dumbfounded, spellbound by the story.

Miss Hunt played with her ring.

'Do you think opals really bring bad luck for that reason, Mr Jennings?' she said at last. 'If you do, do please destroy the stone!'

Mr Jennings took a sharp iron paperweight from the table and hammered gently at the opal until it shattered into shimmering pearly shards.

THE MAN ON THE BOTTLE

Melanchthon was dancing with the little pipistrelle, who had her head downwards and her feet in the air.

With her wings folded across her body, and holding up a big gold ring in her stiff claws, as if to show that she was hanging down from something, she looked altogether peculiar, and the effect on Melanchthon must have been quite remarkable, since he was obliged to gaze through the ring all the time as they danced: it was precisely at his eye-level.

The bat costume was one of the most original fancy-dresses at the Persian prince's ball, – but, to be sure, also one of the most ugly.

Even His Serene Highness Mohammed Daryash-Koh, the host of this occasion, had noticed it.

'I know you, you lovely mask,' he had whispered to her – to the great amusement of the bystanders who overheard.

'I'm sure it's the little marquise, the princess's intimate friend,' hazarded a Dutch burgher, dressed Rembrandt-style – it couldn't be anyone else; she knew every corner of the palace, so she said, and earlier, when several gentlemen had had the 'cool' idea of ordering the old chamberlain to fetch them torches and padded boots so that they could go snowballing in the park, she had eagerly joined in the wild escapade. He would even bet that he had caught a glimpse of a certain hyacinth bracelet on her wrist.

'Oh, how *interesting*,' joined in a blue butterfly, 'couldn't Melanchthon there *possibly* ask a few *tactful* questions about Graf de Faast, who seems to be so very popular with the princess these days?'

'Watch out, don't talk so loud,' the burgher interrupted. 'It's a good thing they're playing the end of the waltz *fortissimo*: the prince was standing behind you just a moment ago!'

'Yes, yes, it's best not to talk about these things,' advised an Egyptian Anubis in a whisper. 'The jealousy of these asiatics has no limits, and there's probably more to burn in the palace than we all think. Graf de Faast has been playing with fire for too long already, and if Daryash-Koh knew. . .'

A rough, tousled figure representing a coil of rope elbowed his way through the group of masks, trying to avoid the attentions of a Greek warrior in shiny armour. The crowd gazed blankly after them as they sped off rubber-soled across the lightly-polished stone flags.

'Wouldn't *you* be frightened of being chopped in two, Mynher Dontgeddit, if *you* were the Gordian Knot and you knew that Alexander the Great was right behind you?' mocked the inverted bat, tapping the solemn Dutchman's nose with her fan.

'Oho, my dear mylady Pipistrelle,' joked Mephisto, immensely tall, with tail and horse's hoof. 'What a pity, what a real pity that we can only see you with your pretty feet in the air when you're dressed as a bat!'

Someone burst into a roar of laughter.

They all looked round and saw a fat old man with padded breeches and an ox's head.

'Ah, the retired Vice-President of the Chamber of Commerce has laughed,' observed the devil drily.

A muffled tone rings out, and an executioner in the red cloak of the Westphalian *vehmgericht* positions himself in the middle of the huge ballroom, leaning on his glittering axe and swinging a bronze bell in one hand.

The masks pour out from loggias and alcoves: harlequins, rose maidens, cannibals, ibises, pusses in boots, fives of spades, Chinese ladies, German poets sporting a label:'forty winks', Don Quixotes, 17th-century knights, columbines, bajadères and dominoes of every colour.

The red executioner distributes small rectangular slips of ivory among the crowd.

'Ah, programmes for the show!'

The Man in the Bottle
Marionette Comedy after Aubrey Beardsley
by Prince Mohammed Daryash-Koh
Cast:
The Man in the Bottle – Miguel Graf de Faast
The Man on the Bottle – Prince Mohammed Daryash-
Koh
The Lady in the Palanquin – x x x
Vampires, Marionettes, Hunchbacks, Apes, Musicians
Scene:
A tiger's open jaws

'What's that? The prince himself wrote it?'

'A scene from the Arabian Nights, perhaps?'

'Who's playing the Lady in the Palanquin, then?' ask several voices filled with curiosity.

'Oh, I'm sure we'll have some *simply amazing* surprises in store for us,' twitters a petite figure swamped in ermine, her arm linked with an abbé: do you know, the pierrot I was dancing the tarantella with earlier, that was Graf de Faast, who's going to play the man in the bottle, and he told me *lots* of things - the marionettes are going to be *awfully* weird, but only for those who know, you know, and the prince himself has sent to Hamburg ... for an *elephant* – - but you're not listening to me!' And she angrily drops her companion's arm and trips away.

Through the wide double doors yet more masks throng into the hall out of adjacent rooms, milling about in the middle of the floor with the random beauty of an ever-changing kaleidoscope, or assembling in groups by the walls to admire the marvellous Ghirlandaio frescoes that cover the walls with fairy-tale landscapes right up to the blue-painted, star-studded ceiling. The hall lies spread out like a multi-coloured island, washed by the waves of rain-bow fantasy which, once upon a time awakened in the joyful imaginings of artists, now whisper a language slow, simple, but barely comprehensible to today's frenetic souls.

Flunkeys appear, bearing refreshments in silver goblets for the light-hearted surge of merrymakers, – sorbet and wine. Chairs are brought, and set in the window bays.

Then with a grating noise the wall at one end of the room parts to reveal a stage, which trundles forward out of the darkness carrying a set blazed reddish-brown and yellow, with white-painted teeth above and below: stylised tiger-jaws, yawning wide.

In the middle there stands a vast rounded bottle made of glass a foot thick, almost twelve feet high, and very capacious. Pink silk curtains form a backdrop. The colossal ebony doors of the hall fly open, and with majestic tread an elephant enters, ornamented with gold and jewels; on his neck the executioner, guiding him with the haft of his axe.

From the points of the animal's tusks chains of amethysts swing in unison with the gentle waving of peacock feath-ers.

Gold-embroidered mats edged with raisin-coloured tas-sels hang from his haunches to the ground.

With his mighty forehead encased in a network of glittering jewels the elephant strides unconcerned across the ballroom.

The masks crowd round him in droves, cheering the gaily attired group of elegant actors riding in the howdah on his back: Prince Daryash-Koh in a turban fastened with a heron's-bill clasp, Graf de Faast next to him as Pierrot, marionettes and musicians stiff and wooden as dolls.

The elephant has reached the stage, and lifts each player down one by one with his trunk. Applause and whoops of approval as he picks up Pierrot and deposits him through the neck of the great bottle, closes the metal lid and sets the prince on the top.

The musicians arrange themselves in a semicircle and produce strange, elongated, spectral-looking instruments.

The elephant gazes earnestly at them, turns slowly, and lumbers off back to the entrance, the masks meanwhile hanging on to his tusks, wildly and noisily excited like rowdy children, clutching at his trunk and ears, trying to hold him back. The elephant scarcely feels them.

The performance begins. Gentle music can be heard, rising, it seems, from somewhere out of the floor.

The marionettes and the doll-orchestra remain immovable, like wax figures.

The flautist stares up at the roof with blank expression and glazed eyes. The conductor, in rococo costume of wig and feathered hat stands as if listening, her baton raised in the air, and a stiffened finger pressed mysteriously to her lips, her features twisted into a lewd and sinister smile.

At the front of the stage the marionettes – a chalkfaced hunchback dwarf, a grinning devil in grey and a sickly-pale singer with brilliant scarlet pouting lips seem conspiratorially locked in the knowledge of some satanic evil, which has left them in a kind of sensual paralysis.

The bristling horror of a catatonic trance oppresses the whole group into immobility.

The only movement comes from Pierrot in the bottle, ceaselessly waving his conical felt hat, bowing and occasionally offering up a flourished greeting to the Persian prince, sitting quietly cross-legged on top of the lid on the bottle.

Pierrot's facial contortions and grotesque capers arouse great merriment among the spectators.

The thick glass of the bottle distorts his appearance in the strangest ways: sometimes his eyes bulge out and glitter strangely, then again they vanish altogether, and he is all forehead and chin, until his head suddenly splits into three.

Sometimes he looks fat and puffed-up, then again as thin as a skeleton, with long spidery legs, until just as suddenly his belly explodes into a great round ball.

Every one of the spectators has a different view of him, depending on the way his image strikes through the glass.

At short intervals, without any recognisably logical sequence, an eerie momentary life invades the static figures before they sink back into their former corpse-like rigidity, as if the image is capable of jumping from one attitude to another across dead space, like the hands of a turret-clock as it ticks from one minute to the next.

At one point, all in unison and with a snap of the knees, the whole group leaps sideways in three spectral bounds towards the bottle, while in the background a stunted and misshapen child writhes in abandoned agony.

One of the musicians – a bashkir with wild lidless stare and bulbous skull – wags his head to the movement, and with a leer of frightful depravity spreads his fingers, lean and horrible, knobbed like drumsticks at the tips, as waxen symbols of some nameless corruption.

Then again, the singer is joined by a fantastically attired female androgyne in a pair of long, bedraggled-looking lace pantaloons, who bounds up to her and then freezes into the attitude of a half-completed dance step.

A welcome release from the tension generated by these periods of immobility was afforded by the arrival on the scene of an enclosed sandalwood litter that appeared, borne on the shoulders of two Moors, from behind the pink hangings of the backdrop, and which was set down close to the bottle, itself now suddenly illuminated from above by a pale lunar light.

The spectators were divided, so to speak, into two camps. One group, struck speechless and immobile, stood hypnotised by the fancifully mysterious, vampire-like antics of the marionettes, who diffused a demonic aura of poisonous and indefinable lasciviousness about them. The remainder, too coarse to be affected by such shocks to the spirit, could do nothing but laugh uproariously at the comic antics of the man in the bottle.

To be sure, he had given up his merry dance, but his behaviour now seemed to them to be no less amusing.

He was evidently trying, by every possible means, to attract the attention of the prince, who was still sitting on the stopper of the bottle, to something that seemed to him to be of particular importance.

He was banging on the glass, jumping up against it even, as if he were trying to break it, or even to turn the bottle over on its side.

At the same time he seemed to be shouting out loud, though of course not a sound was able to penetrate the foot-thick glass.

Pierrot's pantomimic attitudes and gestures were answered from time to time by the Persian with a smile, or sometimes with a finger pointed to the litter.

The curiosity of the audience reached fever pitch as they clearly saw on one of these occasions how Pierrot kept his face pressed up to the glass, as if to make out something through the window of the litter, suddenly, like a madman, clapped his hands to his head as if he had caught sight of a horror, and then fell to his knees tearing his hair. Then he jumped up, and started running round and round inside the bottle so fast that through the distortions of the glass all you could see most of the time was a bright butterfly of cloth.

The spectators were at a loss to understand what the 'Lady in the Palanquin' had to do with it; they were conscious of a white face pressed up against the window of the litter, gazing fixedly at the bottle, but everything else was shrouded in shadow, and they could only guess.

'What on earth is all this about?' whispered the blue domino, clinging more tightly to Mephistopheles.

Opinions were exchanged in an excited undertone.

'Well, the play doesn't actually *mean* anything – only things you can't think about, which affect your emotions directly,' suggested a salamander, 'and just as there are people who get an erotic kick out of watching the watery secretions oozing out of bloodless corpses and can't help an orgasmic shriek or two, there are surely others . . .'

'That's all very well, pain and pleasure grow on the same branch,' interrupted the bat, 'but believe me, I'm altogether keyed up, there's something so unspeakably awful in the air and I can't shake it off: it keeps coming over me and trying to suffocate me. Do you think it's the play? But no, I think it's coming from the prince. Why is he sitting up there on the top, looking so unconcerned? And yet every now and then his face twitches! There's something going on here, for sure.'

'I believe I can think of a certain symbolic significance, which corresponds quite well with what you have said,' chimed in Melanchthon. 'The man in the bottle is undoubtedly an expression of the soul trapped within the human body and forced to watch helplessly as the physical senses, which are represented by the marionettes, indulge their lusts, and as everything hurtles towards irresistible corruption in sin.'

A burst of laughter and applause cut him short.

Pierrot was crouching in the bottom of the bottle clutching at his neck with contorted fingers. Then with gaping mouth he pointed in desperation in turn at his chest and then at a point somewhere above him, finally clasping his hands in supplication, as if begging for something from his audience.

'He wants a drink – look at that: such a big bottle and no champers in it – give him a drink you dolls!' called out one spectator.

Everyone laughed and clapped their hands in approval.

Pierrot jumped up again, tore his shirt wide open, stumbled and fell full length on the bottom of the glass.

'Bravo, bravo, Pierrot, well played; da capo, da capo,' howled the crowd.

But when the fellow remained quite still and made no effort to continue the scene, the applause gradually died down, and people's attention shifted to the marionettes.

These were still standing in the same weird poses they

had earlier assumed, but now there was a kind of tautness in their attitude that had not been there before. It seemed as if they were waiting on some kind of cue.

At length the hunchbacked dwarf with the chalked face cautiously swivelled his eyes towards Prince Daryash-Koh.

Not a muscle moved on the Persian. His features seemed to have collapsed.

At last one of the Moors emerged from among the figures in the background, walked circumspectly up to the litter and opened the door.

And then something altogether singular occurred.

A naked female body fell stiffly from the opening and landed with a dull smack on the floor.

There was an instant of total silence, and then a thousand voices all started at once. The whole of the great hall was in uproar.

'What is it? What's happened?'

Marionettes, apes, musicians – everyone sprang to life; masks leaped up onto the stage.

The princess, wife of Daryash-Koh, lay there on the floor, quite naked, tied to a steel grid. The places where the cords cut into her flesh were suffused blue.

A silken gag had been tied across her mouth.

Indescribable horror rendered every muscle lame.

'Pierrot!' shrieked a voice suddenly – 'Pierrot!' – Wild, unfocussed terror stabbed at every heart.

'Where is the prince?'

In the midst of the tumult the Persian had vanished.

Melanchthon had already clambered up onto the devil's shoulders; in vain – the stopper was immovable, and the little air-ventilator had been . . . *screwed down tight!*

'Smash the sides, come on, quickly!'

The Dutch burgher had torn the axe from the red executioner's hands and was on the stage in a bound.

As the blows fell the glass gave out the sound of a cracked bell – a ghastly noise.

Deep cracks split across the glass like streaks of white lightning; the edge of the axe-blade peeled and burred.

Then, at last . . . the bottle shattered.

Inside lay Graf de Faast, choked to death, his fingers knotted against his chest.

With noiseless pinions the vast black harbingers of horror swept invisibly through the ballroom.

BLAMOL

In truth, without deceit,
I say to you surely
As it is below, so is it above.
Tabula Smaragdina

The old cuttlefish was resting on a thick Blue Book that
had come from a vessel that had sunk, and was slowly
taking in the printed characters.

Landlubbers have absolutely no idea how busy a cuttlefish is all day.

This one had devoted himself wholeheartedly to medicine, and all day long, from morning to night, two poor
little starfish were obliged to help him turn the pages,
because they owed him so much money.

Around his corpulence, just where other people keep
their waists, he wore a golden pince-nez: another piece of
marine loot. The lenses were forced wide apart on either
side, giving anyone who might look through them a
disagreeably dizzy sensation.

All around was quiet.

Suddenly an octopus came lunging up, its baggy snout
pointing eagerly ahead, its arms trailing in its wake like
nothing so much as a bundle of sticks. It settled down
beside the book, and waited for the old fellow to look up
before composing an elaborate greeting and unwrapping a
tin box from amongst its arms. 'The violet polyp from
Turbot Alley, I presume,' observed old Sepia graciously.
'Yes, that's right, I knew your mother well, née von
Octopus. (I say, Perch, just fetch me the *Almanach de
Gophalopoda*, will you.) Now, what can I do for you,
young polyp?'

'The inscription – read what it says,' oozed the other,
embarrassed, pointing to the tin box. He had a rather slimy
way of saying things.

The cuttlefish stared hard at the box, like a prosecuting counsel, his eyes popping out.

'What is this I see – Blamol? This is a priceless find. Surely it comes from the Christmas Steamer that ran aground? Blamol! The new miracle cure – the more you take, the healthier you get!

'This must be opened at once: Perch, just dart off to the two lobsters over there, will you – you know, Coral Bank, Second Branch, the Scissors brothers – and hurry!'

The green sea-lily, who resided nearby, rushed over the moment she heard about the new medicine – oh, she *really would* like to try some, really and truly, she'd give *anything!*

And she undulated her several hundred tentacles in captivatingly languorous fashion, riveting everyone's eye upon her.

Sharks alive, was she beautiful! A big mouth, for sure, but that's often what makes a lady so exciting.

They were all gaping at her, so they missed the arrival of the two lobsters who were already busy at the tin, chattering to each other in their harsh, outlandish dialect. With a final gentle tap the tin fell apart.

Like a shower of hail the white pills swirled out and, lighter than cork, shot upwards and vanished.

'Catch them, catch them!' came the cry, and they all fell over in their haste, but none was quick enough. Only the lily was lucky enough to secure a single pill and she hastily stuffed it into her mouth.

Indignation all round: the least the Scissors brothers deserved was a box on the ear.

'You, Perch, I suppose you couldn't manage to watch what was going on? What's the point of your being my assistant?'

Everyone was left to swear and argue – all except for the octopus who, speechless with rage, was hammering away at a mussel with its clenched tentacles, enough to make the pearls squeak.

Suddenly there was a general silence: look at the lily!

She must have suffered a stroke: rigid and quite unable

to move, with her tentacles stiffly extended, she could be heard gently whimpering.

The cuttlefish pulsed importantly over to her and commenced his examination with a mysterious air. With the aid of a pebble he palpated a tentacle or two and then probed further in. (Hm, hm, – Babynski's Reaction: disruption of the Pyramidal Channels.) Then with the edge of his wing he stroked the lily a few times across her cup, his eyes taking on as he did so an intense and penetrating quality. Finally, puffing himself up, he said in a grave tone: 'Lateral Chord Sclerosis – the lady is paralysed.'

'Is there anything we can do? What is your opinion? Please just help her – I'll go to the chemist's', cried the good-natured seahorse.

'Help? Are you mad? Do you think I studied medicine in order to effect cures?' The cuttlefish was getting angrier. 'It seems to me you think I'm a barber. Are you trying to make fun of me? Perch, my hat and stick, if you please!'

One after another they all dispersed. 'The things that can happen to you in this life. It's awful, don't you think?'

The place emptied, soon leaving the perch grumpily casting about, looking for anything the others might have lost or forgotten.

Night descended upon the seabed. The rays of light, of which none knew whence they came nor whither they went, shimmered in the green water like a veil, tired, as though at the limit of exhaustion.

The poor sea-lily lay immobile, gazing at them with a heart full of bitterness as they rose and vanished into the distance far above. Yesterday at this time she had been fast asleep, curled up safely into a ball, and now – to have to die on the street, like a mere . . . animal! Little pearls of air beaded her brow. And tomorrow was Christmas!

She fell to thinking about her husband, gadding about somewhere far away. Three months it was now since she had become a seagrass-widow. Really, it would have been no surprise if she had been unfaithful to him.

90

Oh, if only the seahorse had stayed with her!

She was so afraid!

It was getting so dark you could hardly see your own feelers in front of you.

Broad-shouldered night crept out from behind the stones and algae, devouring the pale shadows of the coral banks. Black shapes glided out like ghosts, with eyes aflame and luminously violet fins. Fishes of the Night! Hideous rays and sea-devils, going about their nefarious business in the darkness, lying murderously in wait amidst the wreckage of ships.

Stealthily, shiftily, mussels beckon to the belated traveller, inviting him all unwary to join in some gruesome vice amidst the soft pillows that can be glimpsed between their gently parted shells.

In the distance a dogfish barks.

Suddenly, a bright light flashes through the algal ribbons: a shining medusa appears, guiding some drunken revellers homewards – a pair of slick eels, with a couple of moray sluts twined round their fins. Two young salmon, gaudy in silver, have stopped to gaze at this scene of depraved intoxication. A dissolute verse can be heard . . .

> Down where the green weed grew
> I asked when I had met her
> Did she want me to screw
> Her? 'Yes, oh yes, you'd better.'
> So down she bent
> And off I went
> Right where the green weed grew . . .

'Out of my way, bloody salmon!' roars one of the eels, interrupting the song.

Silversides bridles: Shut your trap! You'd do well to watch your language. Just because you think you're the only lot who were born on the right side of the Danube . . .'

'Shh, shh,' the medusa pleads, 'watch your tongues, look who's over there!'

They all fall quiet and gaze with some awe at a small group of frail, colourless figures making prim progress along the way.

'Lancelets' someone whispers.

'? ? ? ?'

'Oh, very hoity-toity they are, Counsellors, diplomats and the like. Born to it. Real marvels of nature – no brain, no backbone: quite spineless.'

There ensues a minute or two of silent amazement before everyone swims away, this time quite peaceably.

The noises die away. Absolute silence descends.

Time passes. Midnight, the witching hour.

Did we hear voices? Not shrimps, surely, at this time of night?

It's the Night Patrol: police crabs!

What a noise they make with their armoured legs as they crunch across the sand, dragging their captives off to a place of security.

Woe betide anyone who falls into their clutches: no crime escapes them, and their lies stand on oath before the law.

Even the electric ray turns pale at their approach.

Lily's heart misses a beat in terror: here she is, a defenceless lady, out in the open! What if they catch sight of her? They'll drag her up before the beak in front of that old perjurer of a crab, the biggest crook in the sea, and then . . . and then . . .

Here they come, getting closer – they're just a step away; the cruel talons of ruin and disgrace are on the point of encircling her waist with their iron grip.

Suddenly the dark water shivers, the coral branches creak and shake like seaweed and a pale glow illumines the scene from afar.

Crabs, rays, sea-devils dart and scatter across the sand, pieces of rock break away and swirl up in the current.

A bluish, smoothly moving wall as big as all the world comes flying through the waters.

Nearer and nearer comes the phosphorescent light, the gigantic glowing wing of *Tintorera*, the demon of annihilation, comes sweeping up, stirring fiery chasm-deep whirlpools in the foaming water.

Everything becomes caught up in the spinning eddies. The lily flies vertiginously up and down again over a landscape of emerald froth. Where now are the crabs, where the shame and dread? Raging destruction has come storming through the world, a bacchanal of death, a glorious dance for the prize of a soul.

The senses expire like a smoking flame.

Then next a frightful shuddering jolt, the eddies stand in the water, but continue to spin faster and faster, flinging down on to the sea floor everything they had previously torn up.

Many a fine armoured piece meets its Waterloo there.

When at last the lily awoke from her fainting fall she found herself lying on a bed of soft algae.

The gentle seahorse (who had taken the day off from work) was bending over her.

A cool morning stream fanned her face, and she looked up. She could hear the cackling of goose-barnacles and the cheerful bleating of a lamprey.

'You are quite safe here in my little house in the country' replied the seahorse to her look of enquiry, and gazing deep into her eyes. 'Please rest a little more, dear lady, it will do you good.'

But she could not, for all she tried. An indescribable feeling of nausea overwhelmed her.

'What a storm that was last night – my head is still swimming from all the commotion', went on the seahorse chattily. 'By the way, can I tempt you to a spot of blubber – a really nice fat piece of juicy sailor-blubber?'

At the mere mention of the word the lily felt so ill that she was obliged to clamp her lips tight shut. But it was no use. She began to retch (the seahorse turned his head discreetly to one side), and in a moment had brought up the Blamol pill which, quite undigested, floated and vanished upwards in a cloud of bubbles.

Thank God the seahorse hadn't seen it.

The invalid suddenly felt as right as rain again.

She curled herself up with contentment.

Wonder of wonders! She could curl up again, could move her limbs about, as before.

Ecstasy upon ecstasy!

The seahorse could feel bubbles of joy pricking his eyes. 'Christmas, it's really Christmas today!' he rejoiced. 'I must tell the cuttlefish at once: in the meanwhile you must have a really good long sleep.'

'What do you find so remarkable about the lily's sudden recovery, my dear Seahorse?' asked the cuttlefish, with a condescending smile. 'You are an enthusiast, my young friend. As a matter of principle I don't usually discuss medical matters with non-professionals (bring up a chair, Perch, for the gentleman), but I'll make an exception this time, and endeavour to match my mode of expression to your level of understanding as far as I can. So, you consider Blamol to be a poison, and you attribute the paralysis to its effects. What a mistake! I might add, by the way, that Blamol is now altogether passé, it is yesterday's panacea; today we usually recommend Idiotine Chloride: medical science strides eternally onwards. That the illness should have coincided with swallowing the pill was pure coincidence – it's well known that everything that happens in the world is coincidence – for in the first place Lateral Chord Sclerosis has a quite different set of causes (though discretion forbids me to name them), and secondly, Blamol works, like all such agents, not when you take it, but only when you spit it out – and then of course it's bound to be beneficial in its effects.

And finally, as far as the cure is concerned, well, here we have a clear case of autosuggestion. In reality, - and by 'reality' I mean what Kant called the *'thing in itself'* – in reality the lady is just as ill as she was yesterday: she just

94

doesn't notice it. It is precisely in the case of those with inferior mental powers that autosuggestion works so effectively. Of course I'm not implying anything by saying this — you know how highly I esteem the little woman at home:

> 'Give all honour to the ladies,
> They plait and weave . . .'
>
> as Schiller puts it.

But now, my young friend, enough of this, it will simply upset you unnecessarily. A propos - you will of course do me the honour? It is Christmas and — I'm getting married.'

'Who is he marrying, then?' he asked the perch on the way out. 'You don't say — the blue mussel? But why not, though — just another one in it for the money.'

When, that evening, the lily arrived, somewhat late but with a glowing complexion, and leaning on the seahorse's fin, the congratulations were without end. Everyone gave her a hug, and even the veiled snails and the cockles who were acting as bridesmaids put their maidenly timidity aside in the warmth of their hearts.

It was a magnificent occasion, as only the rich can provide — the blue mussel's parents had millions after all, and they had even organised some phosphorescent sea-fire.

Four long oyster-banks had been laid out and the feast had lasted well over an hour, yet still more dainty dishes appeared. The perch went on steadily circulating with a glittering decanter (upside down, of course) of hundred year-old air, recovered from the cabin of a sunken wreck.

Everyone had become a little tipsy, and the toasts being drunk to the blue mussel and her bridegroom were being drowned out by the popping and clicking of dead men's fingers and the clatter of razorshells.

The seahorse and the lily were sitting at the far end of the table, quite in the shadows, hardly noticing their surroundings. From time to time he would squeeze one or other of her tentacles, and in return she rewarded him with a glance full of ardour.

Towards the end of the meal the band struck up with a song:

> A joke, a kiss
> For a *married* Miss
> Is utter bliss;
> It's quite what's done
> When you're having fun–
> But he's got to be young . . .

And their table-companions exchanged a sly wink. It would have been impossible not to suppose that everyone had their own ideas about what sort of liaisons were being quietly arranged here.

THE TRUTH-DROP

The ghostly light of dawn was just feeling its way through the dirty streets, breathing a dully shimmering fog against the walls of the houses. Four in the morning! And Hlavata Ohrringle was still awake, pacing back and forth in his room.

To have had in your possession for decades a phial of colourless liquid, which you know for certain has some secret quality; that, taken at a specific moment for instance it may have the capacity to endow you with magical abilities, yet not to be in any position to comprehend the secret — such an idea is depressing and painful. But to see the veil lifted, suddenly, and all at a once, must be exciting and would surely keep you awake.

Hlavata Ohrringle had often picked up the phial in the evening, shaken it, held it up to the light and sniffed at its contents. Over and over again he had turned over the pages of the old folios, which according to hints in his great-grandfather's will were supposed to offer some kind of explanation, and every time he had gone to bed, keyed up, without ever finding anything out. There was just one odd thing: on those occasions he always had the same dream — a landscape of purple mountains with an oriental monastery in the centre, and a golden roof on which stood, in paralysed immobility, a corpse holding a book in its hand. Then, as the cover of the book slowly revealed, a sentence written in Chaldaean letters appeared: 'Stay on your appointed path, and be steadfast.'

And then today, today at last, after such long and fruitless pondering, Hlavata Ohrringle had found that the concealing shell of the secret had as it were split open before his soul's eye, just as a nutshell bursts under the influence of heat.

A passage in one of the treatises which he had overlooked up until now, because it occurred right at the beginning in the introduction, offered the solution precisely. The liquid was what was called an Alchemistical Particular. That was it! An Alchemistical Particular! But the properties of the liquor were odd, and apparently so valueless by modern standards. One drop, suspended between two metal points, would after a few minutes assume the form of a mathematically exact sphere. Interesting – very interesting, that there indeed existed a material which did in fact permit the formation of such a perfect shape; but what else was there? Surely that couldn't be all?

And it wasn't all. Hlavata Ohrringle (who was a true bookworm) soon found a description of this wonderfully valuable material in another folio volume.

Here the sense ran that, if it should prove possible to produce a spherical form in a geometrically correct sense, such things might be glimpsed in its reflection as would surely be a source of great astonishment. The whole astral universe - that spiritual space that underlies our own, as action does intent, or deed decision – might then be perceptible, even if sometimes only in symbolic form. It would be a round eye, seeing in every possible direction into the farthest recesses of space, and arranging, according to laws of surface tension incomprehensible to us, all mirror-images over and beside one another.

Hlavata Ohrringle had made all his preparations, had screwed his metal needle-points into a support, and with infinite care had introduced his drop of liquid between them. Now he could barely contain his impatience for daybreak, and to commence his experiment in the light of dawn. Restlessly he strode backwards and forwards, flung himself into a chair, and looked again at the clock. Still only a quarter past four, dammit!

He leafed through the calender to find out when the sun would rise. And as it so happened today was a Lady Day – and Lady Days are so portentous.

At last the light seemed bright enough. He picked up his magnifying glass and gazed at the drop, glistening between its silvery needle-points.

At first he could see nothing but images of the things that cluttered his room: his writing desk with its lid decorated with painted stars, the books scattered about, the white globe of the lamp and the old gown hanging on the window-catch – and a tiny patch of pink sky, glowing through the panes. But after a moment a dark green hue spread over the drop's surface, swallowing up all these reflections. Landscapes appeared, of basalt rocks, yawning caves and grottoes; fantastical vegetation stretched out, crouched, as if ready to strike; strange arborescent shapes extended great billowing glass-green transparent leaves. The landscape glowed with its own light: it was a scene set in the deep ocean.

A long white patch appeared, becoming more clearly defined and gaining in shape: a drowned corpse, a naked woman, head down, her feet caught in a tangle of stems, hung in the green water. Suddenly a colourless lump, its eyes on stalks and a mass of barbels concealing its hideous mouth, detached itself from the shadow of the rocks and darted towards the body. A second one sped after it.

The first of these monsters had torn the remains apart, and had itself been caught by the other so quickly, that Hlavata Ohrringle could not catch every detail. With a gasp of excitement he bent closer over the glass – but his breath had already clouded the picture and in a moment it vanished completely. It was no use: no effort, no amount of patient waiting could recover the scene, and the drop reflected nothing more than the glorious sun, as it rose above the shimmering haze of the sooty gables.

II

Hlavata Ohrringle had returned from a visit to the outskirts of town with a worried expression. He needed to collect his thoughts. He had been to see an old adherent of the Rosicrucian Order, a certain Eckstein, to ask his advice.

The latter listened long and hard, and then said: 'This is a mystery of unequalled profundity. It was in fact I who rediscovered a summary of experiences such as these in the writings of the Cabbalist Rabbi Gikatilla, though of course they were in coded form. What Basilius Valentinus says in his tractatus 'The Triumphal Car of Antimonius' on page 712 is merely symbolic, or anagogic, that is, it may be grasped only by him whose soul has descended into the heart of the divine.' And if Hlavata Ohrringle were really interested in seeing visions in shining objects, then a Japanese crystal ball would be the most suitable. All those that had so far reached Europe were in point of fact actually to be found in the hands of a sinister black magician by the name of Fahlendien in Vienna, but the best explanation of the scene he had witnessed could on the other hand be given by a mad painter called Christopher who was living in Berlin – if he wanted such an explanation.

Of course Ohrringle was far from satisfied by all this, and every day he tried out fresh experiments with his liquid.

These experiments were naturally no secret in the town, and were a regular topic of the day's conversation. Absurd, they said, completely absurd; how could you possibly see *everything* in a spherical mirror? Most things in space lie *behind* one another, so the one just makes the other invisible.

That struck everyone as extremely plausible, so they were all the more astonished to read the entirely contradictory opinion of an English expert in a foreign newspaper. This was to the effect that it was indeed, in theory, altogether possible to see through walls and into closed boxes: you only had to consider X-rays for instance, against which the only defence was lead sheeting.

Every object in the world, when all was said and done, was nothing more, so to speak, than a fine sieve made of swirling atoms: it was only a matter of finding the right form of radiation and there would be no resistance to its transmission.

This newspaper article turned out to be of especial interest in official circles. Rumours of the most peculiar and top secret decrees filtered down into public awareness. Diplomatic orders sent out to all Attachés for example required the immediate transfer of all documents into *lead containers*. There were proposals for a total reorganisation of the provincial police, and with a view to improving the 'secret' police, negotiations had begun with Russia, to import a quantity of bloodhounds in exchange for a number of domestic *Schweinehunde* surplus to requirements, and so on.

Of course, Hlavata Ohrringle was kept under strict surveillance: and the stricter it was, the more pleased he looked when he went out for a walk. And when one day he appeared on the Esplanade with a positively broad grin on his face the authorities decided to take the most ruthless action, especially as it had become apparent that he only smiled when diplomats were the subject under discussion; indeed, when asked what he thought of the art of diplomacy, he had reported that a swindle could never last indefinitely.

And one day (it was another Lady Day), just when he was sitting looking at one of his mysterious drops, Hlavata Ohrringle was arrested, and taken into custody on a charge of multiple matricide.

His strange liquid was confiscated and turned over for examination to the Department of Forensic Chemistry.

This was bound to be a good development, since now, without question, the truth about diplomats is bound to come out into the open.

- Ahem – I repeat: it *will* come out into the open.

DR. CINDERELLA'S PLANTS

Do you see the little blackened bronze statue over there between the two lamps? That has been the cause of all the weird experiences I have had in recent years.

These phantom perturbations which have so drained my energy are all links in a chain which, if I pursue it back into the past, comes back every time to the same starting point: the bronze.

If I pretend to myself that there may be other causes of my anxieties, the image nevertheless recurs to me, like another milestone along the road.

But where this road is leading me – to ultimate illumination or to ever-increasing horror – I have no desire to know, wishing only to cling on to those occasions when for a few days I feel relief from my doom and can sense freedom until I am overcome by the next shock.

I unearthed the thing in the desert sands of Thebes one day as I was prodding about with my stick, and from the very first moment, as I was examining it more closely, I was struck with a morbid curiosity to know what the image might signify – I have never wanted to know anything quite so urgently.

In the beginning I would ask every explorer I met, but without success. Only one old Arabian collector seemed to have some idea about what it meant.

'A representation of an Egyptian hieroglyph,' he proposed; the unusual position of the arms of the figure must indicate some kind of mysterious ecstatic state.

I took the bronze with me back to Europe, and hardly an evening went by without my falling into the most remarkable reveries about its mystery.

An uncanny feeling would come over me on these occasions as I brooded on some poisonous and malevolent presence which was threatening, with malicious relish, to break out of its lifeless cocoon in order to fasten itself leechlike upon me, and to remain, like some incurable disease, as the dark tyrant of my life. Then one day, as I was concerned with quite a different matter, the thought which made sense of the whole riddle struck me with such force, and so unexpectedly, that I staggered under its impact.

Such shafts of illumination strike into our souls like meteors. We know not whence they come: we witness only their white-hot gleam as they fall.

It is almost like a feeling of fear — then — a slight — as — as if some alien ... What am I trying to say?! I'm sorry, sometimes I get so forgetful, especially since I've had to drag this lame leg along. Yes, well, the answer to my brooding thoughts appeared suddenly stark in front of my eyes: *imitation!*

And as if the one word had demolished a wall, I was overcome by the flood-waves of a realisation that that alone must be the key to all the mysteries of our existence.

An uncanny, automatic act of imitation, unconscious, perpetual, the hidden guide of every creature!

An omnipotent, mysterious guide — a masked pilot, silently stepping on board the ship of life in the grey of the dawn. Rising up out of those measureless chasms into which our soul delights to descend when sleep has closed the gates of day! And perhaps down there in those abysses of disembodied existence there stands the brazen image of a demon willing us to be like him, to shape ourselves in his likeness.

And this word: 'imitate', this brief call from the ether became a road for me, and I set out on it at that same moment. I took up the pose, raised both arms above my head in imitation of the statue, and lowered my fingers until the nails just brushed my scalp.

Nothing happened.

No change, either within me or round about me.

So as to make no mistake in my pose I looked more

closely at the figure, and saw that the eyes were closed, as if in sleep.

I decided that I had had enough, broke off the exercise, and put further action off until nightfall. When that came I stilled the ticking of the clocks and lay down, reassuming the position of my arms and hands.

A few minutes passed in this state, but I cannot believe that I could have fallen asleep.

Suddenly there seemed to come echoing out from somewhere inside me a sound, as of a huge stone rumbling down into the depths.

And as if my consciousness were tumbling after it down a monstrous staircase, bouncing two, four, then eight and ever more steps at a time, my memory leaped back through my life, and the spectre of apparent death cloaked itself about me.

What then happened I will not say: none can say it.

People laugh at the idea that the Egyptians and Chaldaeans are supposed to have possessed a magic secret, guarded by uraeus snakes, and never betrayed by any one of the thousands of initiates.

There are no oaths which can possibly bind so securely, we think.

And I, too, thought this once; but in that instant I understood.

It is an event in no way connected with human experience, where perceptions lie as it were one behind another, and there is no oath that binds the tongue – the merest thought of a hint at these things, here on this side, and it is enough to alert the vipers of life into taking aim to strike at your very heart.

So the great secret stays hidden, for it conceals itself and will remain a secret for as long as the world lasts.

But all that is merely incidental to the searing blow which has struck me down for ever. Even someone's superficial fate may be shifted on to a new track if his consciousness can break through the barriers of earthly perception for just one moment.

A fact, of which I am a living example.

Since that night, when I had that out-of-body experience (I can describe it in no other way), the course of my life has changed, and my existence, previously so unhurried, now reels from one inexplicable, horrific experience to another, towards some dark, unfathomable goal.

It is as if a devil's hand is measuring out my periods of lucidity in ever-diminishing quantities, thrusting into my path images of terror which grow in awfulness from one occasion to the next, as if slowly and stealthily to create a new and unheard-of form of madness in me, a form imperceptible to an outsider, unsuspected, known only through the nameless torment of its victim.

In the course of the next few days after the experiment with the hieroglyph I began to experience sensations which I took at first to be hallucinations. In the midst of all the sights and sounds of everyday I would become suddenly aware of strange roaring noises or jarring undertones in my ears, or catch sight of shimmering colours which I had never seen before.

Bizarre figures would appear, unheard and unseen by anyone else, acting out incomprehensible and unfathomable plots in shadowy gloom. They would shift their shapes, lie suddenly still as death, then slither down along the gutters in viscous elongation, or squat stupid and exhausted in dark doorways, as if drained of existence.

This condition of hypersensitive awareness does not persist – it waxes and wanes like the moon.

The steady decline of my interest in others, whose desires and hopes impinge on me only as if from a distance, suggests to me that my soul is engaged upon some dark journey, far far away from the rest of humanity.

At first I allowed these whispering voices filling the edges of my consciousness to lead me along. Now, I am like a beast of burden, strapped firmly into its harness and obliged to follow exactly the path along which I am being driven.

And so one night I was again dragged awake and forced to wander aimlessly through the silent alleyways of the Kleinseite, just for the sake of the impression that the antiquated houses make upon me.

This part of Prague is uncanny, like nowhere else in the world.

The bright light of day never reaches down here, nor yet is it ever quite as dark as night.

A dim, gloomy illumination emanates from somewhere or other, seeping down from the Hradschin on to the roofs of the city below, like a phosphorescent haze. You turn into a narrow lane, and see nothing: only a deathly darkness, until suddenly a spectral ray of light stabs into your eyes from a chink in a shutter, like a long, malevolent needle.

Then a house looms out of the fog – with decayed, drooping shoulders it stares vacantly up into the night sky out of blank lights set into the receding forehead of its sloping roof, like some animal wounded unto death.

Next door, another building leans inquisitively forward, glimmering windows peering down, searching eagerly through the depths of the well down below for any trace of the goldsmith's daughter who drowned there a century ago. And if you walk further on across the uneven cobbles and then suddenly turn to look back, you'll very likely catch sight of a pale and bloated visage staring after you from the corner – not at shoulder height, no, but quite low down, at about the level where you might expect to meet the gaze of a large dog.

There was nobody out in the streets.

Deathly still.

The ancient entries held their lips firmly clamped shut. I turned into Thungasse, where Countess Morzin has her great house.

There in the mist crouched a narrow building, no more than two windows broad, a disagreeable wall with a hectic pallor; and here I was gripped spellbound as I felt my mood of hypersensitivity rising within me.

Under such conditions I act spontaneously, as if driven by another will, and I scarcely know what the next moment will make me do.

So, in this state, I pushed open the door which had been merely standing ajar, and, passing down a passage, descended the stairs to the cellar, all as if I really belonged in this house.

At the bottom, the invisible rein holding me in check was relaxed and I was left standing in the darkness, painfully aware that I had done something entirely without purpose.

Why had I gone down there? Why hadn't I even thought of putting a stop to such a pointless idea? I was ill, patently ill, and I took comfort in the fact that it could be nothing else: the mysterious, uncanny force had nothing to do with it.

But in the next moment I realised that I had opened the door, entered the house and gone down the stairs without once bumping into anything, like someone who knew every step of the way: my hope evaporated on the instant.

My eyes slowly became accustomed to the darkness, and I looked about me.

There on one of the steps of the cellar stairs someone was sitting. How could I have got past without touching him?

I could only see the crouched figure rather indistinctly in the darkness.

A black beard covered a bare chest; the arms were bare too.

Only the legs seemed to be encased in trousers or perhaps a loincloth. There was something fearful about the position of his hands – they were so extraordinarily bent back, almost at right angles to the joint.

I stared at the man for a long time.

He sat there with such corpse-like rigidity that I had the sense that his outline had somehow become etched into the dark background, and that this image would remain until the house itself fell into ruin.

A cold shiver overcame me, and I went on down the twisting passage.

At one point I reached out to touch the wall. My fingers closed upon a splintered wooden trellis, such as creepers are trained on. They seemed indeed to be growing there in great profusion, for I almost got caught up in a maze of stalky tendrils.

The odd thing was that these plants (or whatever they were) felt warm to the touch and full of life – altogether they seemed to have a certain animal quality.

I put my hand out once more, but immediately snatched it back again: this time I had touched a round ball about the size of a walnut, which felt cold and which shrank away on the instant. Was it a beetle?

Just then a light flickered on somewhere, and for a second the wall in front of me was lit up.

Everything I had known of fear and horror up until then was as nothing to this moment.

Every fibre of my being shrieked out in indescribable terror. My paralysed vocal chords gave vent to a silent scream, which struck through me like a shaft of ice.

The entire wall, right up to the ceiling, was festooned with a network of twisted veins, from which hundreds of bulbous berry-eyes gazed out.

The one I had just fingered was still snapping back and forth, giving me a glance full of suspicion.

I felt faint, and staggered on for two or three more steps into the darkness. A cloud of different smells engulfed me, heavy, earthy, reeking of fungus and ailanthus.

My knees gave way and I beat the air about me. A little glowing ring appeared in front of me – the last dying gleam of an oil-lamp which flickered fitfully for a moment.

I leaped towards it and with trembling fingers turned the wick up, just in time to save the tiny sooty flame.

Then I swung round, holding the lamp protectively in front of me.

The room was empty.

On the table, where the lamp had been, there lay a longish object, glittering in the light.

My hand reached out to it, as for a weapon.

But it was no more than a light, crudely-made thing that I picked up.

Nothing moved, and I breathed a sigh of relief. Carefully, so as not to extinguish the flame, I ran the light along the wall. Everywhere the same wooden trellis-work and, as I could now clearly see, overgrown with veins, evidently all patched together, in which blood was coursing.

In amongst them countless eyeballs glistened horribly, sprouting alternately with hideous warty nodules like blackberries, and following me slowly with their gaze as I passed. Eyes of all sizes and colours, from brightly shining irises to the light blue tone of the eye of a dead horse, fixed immovably upwards. Some, shrunken and black, looked like over-ripe nightshade berries. The main stems twisted their way out of jars filled with blood, drawing up their juice by means of some unfathomable process.

I stumbled on shallow dishes filled with whitish fatty lumps in which toadstools were growing covered in a glossy sheen; toadstools of red flesh, that shrank away at a touch.

And all seemed to be parts of living bodies, fitted together with indescribable art, robbed of any human soul, and reduced merely to vegetative organisms.

I could see clearly that they were alive by the way that the pupils in the eyes narrowed when I brought the lamp closer. But who could be the devilish gardener who had planted this horrible orchard?

I remembered the man on the cellar steps.

I reached instinctively into my pocket for a weapon – any weapon – and felt the sharp object I had previously found. It glittered, bleak and scaly: a pine cone assembled out of a multitude of pink human fingernails.

With a shudder I dropped it and clenched my teeth: I must get out, out – even if the thing on the stairs should wake up and set about me!

And I was already on my way past him, ready to thrust him aside, when I realised he was dead, yellow as wax.

From his contorted hands the nails had been wrenched, and incisions in his chest and temples indicated that he had been a subject of dissection. In pushing past him I must have brushed him with my hand – he seemed to slip down a couple of steps towards me and then stood upright, his arms bent upwards, hands touching his forehead.

Just like the Egyptian figure: the same pose, the very same pose!

The lamp smashed to the floor and I knew only that I had flung the door open to the street as the brazen demon of spasmodic cramp closed his fingers round my twitching heart.

Then, half-awake, I realised that the man must have been suspended by cords attached to his elbows: only by that means could he have been brought upright by slipping down the steps; and then, then I felt someone shaking me. 'Come on, the Inspector wants to see you.'

I was taken to a poorly-lit room, tobacco pipes ranged along the wall, a uniform coat hanging on a stand. It was a police station.

An officer was holding me upright.

The Inspector at the table stared past me. 'Have you taken his details?' he murmured.

'He had some visiting cards on him. We've taken those.' I heard the policeman reply.

'What were you up to in Thungasse in front of an open street door?'

Long pause.

'Hey, you!' warned the policeman, giving me a nudge.

I stammered something about a murder in the cellar of the house in Thungasse.

The policeman left the room.

The Inspector, still not bothering to give me a glance, embarked on a long speech, of which I heard very little.

'What are you talking about? Dr. Cinderella is a great scientist – Egyptologist – he is cultivating all sorts of new carnivorous plants – Nepenthes, Droseras and suchlike, I think, I don't know. – You should stay indoors at night.'

A door opened behind me; I turned to face a tall figure with a long heron's bill – an Egyptian Anubis.

The world went black in front of me as Anubis bowed to the Inspector and went up to him, whispering to me as he passed: 'Dr. Cinderella.'

Doctor Cinderella!

At that moment something important from the past came back into my mind and then immediately vanished again.

When I looked at Anubis once again he had become nothing more than an ordinary clerk with something bird-like about his features. He gave me my own visiting cards back. On them was printed:

Dr. Cinderella.

The Inspector suddenly looked straight at me, and I could hear him saying: 'You're the Doctor himself. You should stay at home at night.'

And the clerk led me out. As I went I brushed against the coat hanging on the stand.

It subsided to the floor, leaving the arms hanging.

On the whitewashed wall behind, its shadow raised its arms aloft, as it attempted awkwardly to take up the pose of the Egyptian statuette.

You know, that was my last experience, three weeks ago. I've had a stroke since then: I have two separate sides to my face, and I have to drag my left leg along.

I have looked in vain for that narrow, fevered little house, and down at the station nobody admits to knowing anything about that night.

ST GINGOLPH'S URN

Half-an-hour's walk from St. Gingolph, behind the hills, there is an ancient park, wild and deserted. It's not marked on any map.

The mansion that once stood at its heart must have fallen down centuries ago. The white remains of its foundation walls – they reach scarcely to your knees – project at intervals out of the tall, rampant grass, like the gigantic bleached tooth-stumps of some prehistoric monster.

The earth has unceremoniously buried everything, and the wind has blown it all away: the name of the owners and their coat of arms, the gates and gateways, everything, lock, stock and barrel.

And the sun has glared down on turret and tower, on and on, until everything has slowly fallen into dust, and been wafted away with the vapours of the valley.

So is it that the all-consuming sun treats the things of this earth.

One mouldering stone urn, standing deep in cypress shade, has survived in the park, the last remains of a forgotten era. The dark boughs have sheltered it from the storms.

I once sat down in the grass beside this urn, and was listening to the idle chatter of the crows in the treetops when some clouds suddenly laid a hand across the sun and the light of heaven went out, as if a thousand sad eyes had suddenly closed around me.

I lay still for a long time, hardly moving.

The lowering cypresses stood guard darkly over the urn, which gazed down at me with its weathered stone face, a being without breath or heart, grey and insensible.

And my thoughts slipped down into a sunken realm, full of the sounds of fairy tales and the mysterious timbre of metallic harp-strings; I imagined beribboned children coming with dried twigs and pebbles in their little hands, and standing on tiptoe to throw them into the urn.

And then I pondered long on the reason why this urn had such a heavy lid, like a defiant stone shell, and I felt a strange sensation come over me at the thought of the air inside, and the few poor mouldered objects that it perhaps contained, and how they lay so secretly and without purpose, cut off perhaps for ever from the throbbing life outside.

I tried to move, and felt as if my limbs were locked in sleep while the multicoloured images of the world grew pale around me.

And I dreamed that the cypresses had grown young again, and were swaying imperceptibly in the gentle breeze.

Starlight shimmered on the urn, and the shadow of a huge bare crucifix that towered, dumb and spectral over it, fell like the entry to a dark tunnel across the white nocturnal gleam of the meadow.

The hours ticked by, and here and there bright circles flitted for a few moments across the grass and over the glittering heads of wild fennel, which glowed magically in the light, like coloured metal; sparks struck by the moonlight through the trees as it rose above the brow of the hill.

The park was waiting for something, or someone, who was coming: and when the gravel of the path from the mansion which was itself invisible in deep shadow crunched gently under a footfall, and the air wafted the sound of a rustling dress towards me, it seemed as if the trees all stretched forward, bending down to whisper words of warning to the visitor.

The steps were those of a young mother who had come from the house, and had now thrown herself down at the foot of the cross, embracing its wooden base in an attitude of despair.

Someone else was standing in the shadow of the cross, though, and him she could not see, nor did she suspect his presence. He it was who in the half-light had stolen her sleeping child from its cradle, and now waited for her to come, hour by hour: her husband, driven back home from his far travels by gnawing suspicion and tortured dreams.

He was holding his face pressed to the wood of the cross, and listening with bated breath to the whispered words of her prayer.

He well knew his wife's soul, and the hidden springs of her inner nature, and knew that she would come. To *this* cross. He had seen it all in a dream. She was *bound* to come, to look for her child here.

Like iron to a magnet, as the instinct of the bitch seeks out her lost puppy, so this same enigmatic power will direct a mother's step, even if she were asleep.

As if to warn her the leaves and twigs rustled, and the night dew fell on her hands. But she kept her eyes lowered, her senses were blind for grief and sorrow at the fate of her vanished child.

And so she did not feel that the crucifix was bare, and that it did not carry Him to whom she called, and who had said: go, and sin no more. But instead of the One, he who heard the words of her agony would be a confessor without mercy. And she prayed and prayed, and more and more clearly her supplication formed itself into a confession – Look not, Oh Lord, at my guilt, you forgave that sinner ... And the old branches groaned aloud in their distress and their torment, and grasped at the Listener there behind the cross, and clawed at his cloak – and a blast of wind howled through the park.

Its roaring tore the last traitorous words away, but an ear filled with hatred is not to be deceived by the storm, and in a flash a sure certainty is born out of long-harboured suspicion.

Once more stillness reigned round about.

The supplicant at the cross crouched in a heap, unmoving, as if in deep sleep.

And gently, gently the stone lid began to turn, and the hands of the man glinted pale in the darkness as they crept like monstrous spiders slowly and silently around the edge of the urn.

There was not a sound in the whole park. Paralytic horror stalked throught the darkness.

114

Line by line the stone threads sank and vanished as the lid screwed shut.

Just then a narrow beam of moonlight struck through the thicket and fell upon the ornamental decoration of the urn, glinting from the smooth knob as a horrible glowing eye and staring straight into the man's face with unblinking and malignant gaze.

Feet spurred on by horror and fear fled through the wood, and the cracking of twigs roused the young woman in alarm.

The sounds grew fainter, and died away in the distance.

But she took no notice of them: her heart missed a beat as she heard a tiny sound that had reached her ear in the darkness: an imperceptible, almost inaudible sound, borne as it were on the air.

Was it not a faint whimper? Quite close by?

She stood quite still and strained her ears, biting her lip; her hearing became as acute as an animal's: and she held her breath to suffocation point, yet still her exhalations were like the roar of the tempest. Her heart resounded, and the blood rushed through her veins like a thousand subterranean rivers.

She could hear the scraping of caterpillars under the bark of the trees, and the imperceptible movement of the ears of grass.

And the enigmatic voices of burgeoning internal thoughts, those unborn thoughts that determine the fate of man and bind his will in invisible fetters, but which are yet fainter, fainter by far than the breath of the growing plants, these thoughts began strangely and indefinably to assail her ear.

And all around a cry, a cry of distress, around, above and beneath her, in the air and under the ground.

Her child was crying – somewhere – there, or there, her fingers clenched in mortal anguish – God would let her find him again.

It must be very, very close by – God is just putting her to the test, surely. And the cry sounds nearer, and louder: madness flaps its sable pinions, covering the face of heaven in darkness – her whole brain is just a single aching listening nerve.

Just one single moment of mercy, Oh God, just one moment more, and the child will be found again. In desperation she rushes forward, but the very noise of her first step drowns the faint sound, confuses her ear, and she stops, bewitched, unable to move from her place. She is bound helplessly to the spot, immobile as a stone, for fear of losing the clue.

Again she hears the child: he is crying for her; the moonlight breaks through, lighting up the park, flooding down from the treetops in shimmering streams; and the decoration on the urn glitters like wet mother-of-pearl.

The shadows of the cypresses point: here, here he is, trapped. Break the stone, quick, quick, before he smothers! But the mother does not hear, does not see.

A patch of light has deceived her, and without thinking she has rushed headlong into the bushes, tearing her flesh on the thorns, and trampling through the undergrowth like a maddened beast.

Her shrieks echo dreadfully across the park.

White figures come rushing from the house; sobbing, they catch her hands and in their compassion carry her away.

But the madness has cast its cloak over her, and that same night she is dead.

Her child has suffocated, and nobody found the tiny corpse.

The urn watched over it, until it collapsed into dust.

The old trees fell sick after that night, and slowly they withered, leaving only the cypresses to hold the wake until the present day.

They never spoke a word more, but grew stiff and motionless for grief. But in silence they cursed the wooden crucifix, until the north wind came, tore it out of the ground and flung it down on its face.

The wind would have smashed the urn too in its rage, but that God had forbidden; a stone is always just, and this one had not been any harder than a human heart.

I feel a weight on my chest, which makes me wake up. I look about me, and the space beneath the sky is full of a broken light. The air feels hot and poisonous.

The mountains look as if they are huddled together in alarm, and the outline of every tree stands out with fearful clarity. A few white flecks of foam scud across the water, driven by some mysterious power. The lake is black, yawning below me like the gaping jaws of a monstrous and rabid hound.

A long purple cloud, like nothing I have ever seen before, hangs awesomely motionless above the storm, reaching a spectral arm across the sky.

The dream of the urn still weighs on me like a nightmare, and I sense that it is the arm of the warm wind up there, whose distant hand is groping invisibly about the earth, searching for that stony heart, that was harder even than a rock.

THE RING OF SATURN

One step at a time they came, disciples feeling their way up the circular stair.

Inside the Observatory the darkness came billowing up into the round space, while from above starlight trickled down along the polished brass tubes of the telescope in thin cold streaks. If you turned your head slowly, allowing your gaze to traverse the darkness, you could see it flying off in showers of sparks from the metal pendulums suspended from the roof.

The blackness of the floor swallowed up the glittering drops as they slid off the smooth surface of the shining instruments.

'The Master's concentrating on Saturn today,' said Wijkander after a while, pointing to the great telescope that thrust through the open roof panel like the stiff, damp feeler of a vast golden snail from out of the night sky.

None of the disciples contradicted him: they weren't even surprised when they looked into the eyepiece and found his assertion confirmed.

'It's a complete mystery to me. How can anyone in this near-darkness possibly know what the instrument is pointed at, merely by looking at its position?' said one, bemused.

'How can you be so sure, Axel?'

'I can just sense that the room is filled with the suffocating influence of Saturn, Dr Mohini. Believe me, telescopes really do suck at the stars like leeches, funnelling their rays, visible and invisible, down into the whirling focus of their lenses.

Whoever is prepared, as I have been for a long time now, to stay awake through the night, can learn to detect and to distinguish the fine and imperceptible breath of each star, to note its ebb and flow, and how it can silently insinuate itself into our brains, filling them with changeling intentions; will feel these treacherous forces wrestling in enmity with one another as they seek to command our ship of fortune ... He will learn, too, to dream while awake, and to observe how at certain times of the night the soulless shades of dead planets come sliding into the realm of visibility, eager for life, exchanging mysterious confidences among themselves by means of strangely tentative gestures, instilling an uncertain and indefinable horror into our souls ...

But do turn the lights on — we may easily upset the instruments on the tables in the dark like this, and the Master has never allowed things to get out of place.'

One of the companions found his way to the wall and felt for the switch, his fingertips brushing gently but audibly against the sides of the recess. Then suddenly it was light and the brassy yellow lustre of the telescopes and pendant metal shouted aloud across the emptiness.

The night sky, which until that moment had lain in yielding satin embrace with the window-panes, suddenly leaped away and hid its face far, far above in the icy wastes behind the stars.

'There is the big, round flask, Doctor,' said Wijkander, 'which I spoke to you about yesterday, and which the Master has been using for his latest experiment. And these two metal terminals you see here on the wall supply the alternating current, or Hertz Waves, to envelop the flask in an electric field.

You promised us, Doctor, to maintain an absolute discretion about anything you might witness, and to give us the benefit of your wisdom and experience as a doctor in the mad-house, as far as you can.

Now, when the Master comes up he will suppose himself to be unobserved, and will begin those procedures which I hinted at but cannot explain in more detail. Do you really think that you will be able to remain unaffected by his actions and simply by means of silent observation of his overall behaviour be able to tell us whether madness is altogether out of the question?

On the other hand will you be able to suppress your

scientific prejudices so far as to concede, if necessary, that here is a state of mind unknown to you, the condition of high intoxication known as a Turya Trance - something indeed that science has never seen, but which is certainly not madness?

Will you have the courage openly to admit that, Doctor? You see, it is only our love for the Master and our desire to protect him from harm that has persuaded us to take the grave step of bringing you here and obliging you to witness events that perhaps have never been seen by the eye of an uninitiate.'

Doctor Mohini considered. 'I shall in all honesty do what I can, and be mindful of everything you told me and required of me yesterday, but when I think carefully about it all it puts my head in a spin - can there really be a whole branch of knowledge, a truly secret wisdom, which purports to have explored and conquered such an immeasurably vast field, yet of whose very existence we haven't even heard?

You're speaking there not just about magic, black and white, but making mention also of the secrets of a hidden green realm, and of the invisible inhabitants of a violet world!

You yourself, you say, are engaged in violet magic, – you say that you belong to an ancient fraternity that has preserved its secrets and arcana since the dawn of prehistory.

And you speak of the 'soul' as of something proven! As if it is supposed to be some kind of fine substantive vortex, possessing a precise consciousness!

And not only that – your Master is supposed to have trapped such a soul in that glass jar there, by wrapping it round with your Hertzian oscillation?!

I can't help it, but I find the whole thing, God knows, pure . . .'

Axel Wijkander pushed his chair impatiently aside and strode across to the great telescope, where he applied his eye peevishly to the lens.

'But what more can we say, Dr Mohini?' responded one of the friends at last, with some hesitation. 'It *is* like that: the Master *did* keep a human soul isolated in the flask for a long time; he managed to strip off its constricting layers one at a time, like peeling the skins off an onion, so as to refine its powers, until one day it managed to seep through the glass past the electric field, and escaped!'

At that moment the speaker was interrupted by a loud exclamation, and they all looked up in surprise.

Wijkander gasped for breath: 'A ring – a *jagged* ring, whitish, with holes in it – it's unbelievable, unheard of!' he cried, 'A new ring of Saturn has appeared!'

One after another they looked in the glass with amazement.

Dr Mohini was not an astronomer, and knew neither how to interpret nor to assess the immense significance of such a phenomenon: the formation of a new ring around Saturn. He had scarcely begun to ask his questions when a heavy tread made itself heard ascending the spiral stair. 'For Heaven's sake, get to your places, – turn the light out, the Master's coming!' ordered Wijkander urgently, 'and you, doctor, stay in that alcove, whatever happens, do you hear? If the Master sees you, it's all up!'

A moment later the Observatory was once more dark and silent.

The steps came nearer and nearer, and a figure dressed in a white silk robe appeared and lit a tiny lamp. A bright little circle of light illuminated the table.

'It breaks my heart,' whispered Wijkander to his neighbour. 'Poor, poor Master. See how his face is twisted with sorrow!'

The old man made his way to the telescope where, having applied his eye to the glass, he stood, gazing intently. After a long interval he withdrew and shuffled unsteadily back to the table like a broken man.

'It's getting bigger by the hour!' he groaned, burying his face in his hands in his anguish. 'And now it's growing points: this is frightful!'

Thus he sat for what seemed an age, whilst his followers wept silently in their hiding-places.

Finally he roused himself, and with a movement of sudden decision got up and rolled the flask closer to the telescope. Beside it he placed three objects, whose precise nature it was impossible to define.

Then he kneeled stiffly in the middle of the room, and started to twist and turn, using his arms and torso, into all sorts of odd contorted shapes resembling geometrical figures and angles, while at the same time he started mumbling in a monotone, the most distinguishing feature of which was an occasional long-drawn-out wailing sound.

'Almighty God, have pity on his soul – it's the conjuration of Typhon,' gasped Wijkander in a horrified whisper. 'He's trying to force the escaped soul back from outer space. If he fails, it's suicide; come brothers, when I give the sign it's time to act. And hold on tight to your hearts – even the proximity of Typhon will burst your heart-ventricles!'

The adept was still on his knees, immobile, while the sounds grew ever louder and more plaintive.

The little flame on the table grew dull and began to smoke, glimmering through the room like a burning eye, and it seemed as if its light as it flickered almost imperceptibly was taking on a greenish-violet hue.

The magician ceased his muttering; only the long wails continued at regular intervals, enough to freeze the very marrow of one's bones. There was no other sound. Silence, fearful and portentous, like the gnawing anguish of death.

A change in the atmosphere became apparent, as if everything all round had collapsed into ashes, as if the whole room were hurtling downwards, but in an indefinable direction, ever deeper, down into the suffocating realm of the past.

Then suddenly there is an interruption: a sequence of slithery slapping sounds, as some invisible thing, dripping wet, patters muddily with short, quick steps across the room. Flat shapes of hands, shimmering with a violet glow, materialise on the floor, slipping uncertainly to and fro, searching for something, attempting to raise themselves out of their two-dimensional existence, to embody themselves, before flopping back, exhausted. Pale, shadowy beings, dreadful decerebrated remnants of the dead have detached themselves from the walls and slide about, mindless, purposeless, half conscious and with the stumbling, halting gait of idiotic cripples. They puff their cheeks out with manic, vacant grins – slowly, very slowly and furtively, as if trying to conceal some inexplicable but deadly purpose, or else they stare craftily into space before lunging forwards in a sudden movement, like snakes.

Bloated bodies come floating silently down from the ceiling and then uncoil and crawl away – these are the horrible white spider-forms that inhabit the spheres of suicides and which with mutilated cross-shapes spin the web of the past which grows unceasingly from hour to each succeeding hour.

An icy fear sweeps across the room – the intangible that lies beyond all thought and comprehension, the choking fear of death that has lost its root and origin and no longer rests on any cause, the formless mother of horror.

A dull thud echoes across the floor as Dr Mohini falls dead.

His face has been twisted round back to front; his mouth gapes wide open. Wijkander yells again: 'Keep a tight hold on your hearts, Typhon is . . .' as all at once a cacophony of events erupts.

The great flask shatters into a thousand misshapen shards, and the walls begin to glow with an eerie phosphorescent light. Around the edges of the skylights and in the window-niches an odd form of decomposition has set in, converting the hard stone into a bloated, spongy mass, like the flesh of bloodless, decayed and toothless gums, and licking across the walls and ceilings with the rapidity of a spreading flame.

The adept staggers to his feet, and in his confusion has

seized a sacrificial knife, plunging it into his chest. His acolytes manage to stay his hand, but the damage is done: the deep wound gapes open and life trickles away – they cannot close it up again.

The brilliance of the electric lights has once again taken possession of the circular compass of the Observatory: the spiders, the shadows and the corruption have vanished.

But the flask remains in shattered pieces, there are obvious scorch marks on the floor, and the Master still lies bleeding to death on a mat. They have sought in vain for the knife. Beneath the telescope, limbs contorted, lies the body of Mohini, chest down. His face, twisted upwards, grins grotesquely at the roof reflecting all the horror of death.

The disciples gather round the spot where the Master rests. He gently brushes aside their pleas to stay quiet: 'Let me speak, and do not grieve. No-one can save me now, and my soul longs to complete that which was impossible while it was trapped in my corporeal state.

Did you not see how the breath of corruption has touched this building? Another instant, and it would have become substance, as a fog solidifies into hoar-frost, and the whole Observatory and everything in it would have turned to mould and dust.

Those burns there on the floor were caused by the denizens of the abyss, swollen with hate, desperately trying to reach my soul. And just as these marks you can see are burned into the wood and stone, their other actions would have become visible and permanent if you had not intervened so bravely.

For everything on earth that is, as the fools would have it, 'permanent', was once no more than mere shadow - a ghost, visible or invisible, and is now still nothing more than a *solidified* ghost.

For that reason, everything, be it beautiful or ugly, sublime, good or evil, serene though with death in its heart or alternatively, sad though harbouring secret happiness – all these things have something spectral about them.

It may be only a few who have the gift of detecting the ghostly quality of the world: it is there nevertheless, eternal and unchanging.

Now, it is a basic doctrine of our brotherhood that we should try to scale the precipitous cliffs of life in order to reach that pinnacle where the Great Magician stands with all his mirrors, conjuring up the whole world below out of deceptive reflections.

See, I have wrestled to achieve ultimate wisdom; I have sought out some human existence or other, to kill it in order to examine its soul. I wished to sacrifice some truly useless individual, so I went about among the people, men and women, thinking that such a one would be simple to find.

With the joyous expectation of certainty I visited lawyers, doctors, soldiers – I nearly found one in the ranks of schoolteachers – so very nearly!

But it was always only nearly – there was always some little mark, some tiny secret sign on them, which forced me to loosen my grip.

Then came a moment when at last I found what I was looking for. But it was not an individual: it was a whole group.

It was like uncovering an army of woodlice, sheltering underneath an old pot in the cellar.

Clergywives!

The very thing!

I spied on a whole gaggle of clergywives, watching them as they busied themselves at their 'good works', holding meetings in support of 'education for the benighted classes' or knitting horrible warm stockings and protestant cotton gloves to aid the modesty of poor little piccaninnies, who might otherwise enjoy their God-given nakedness. And then just think how they pester us with their exhortations to save bottle-tops, old corks, paper, bent nails and that sort of rubbish – waste not, want not!

And then when I saw that they were about to hatch out new schemes for yet more missionary societies, and to water down the mysteries of the scriptures with the scourings of their 'moral' sewage, the cup of my fury ran over at last.

One of them, a real flax-blonde 'German' thing – in fact a genuine outgrowth of the rural Slavonic underbrush - was all ready for the chop when I realised that she was – 'great with child' – and Moses' old law obliged me to desist.

I caught another one – ten more – a hundred – and every one of them was in the same interesting condition!

So then I put myself on the alert day and night, always ready to pounce, and at last I managed to lay my hands on one just at the right moment as she was coming out of the maternity ward.

A real silky Saxon pussy that was, with great big blue goose-eyes.

I kept her locked up for another nine months, to be on the safe side, just in case there was anything more to come in the way of parthenogenesis or perhaps budding, such as you get with deep-sea molluscs for instance.

In those moments of her captivity when I was not directly watching her she wrote a great thick book: *Fond Thoughts for our German Daughters on the Occasion of their Reception into Adulthood*. But I managed to intercept it in time and incinerate it in the oxy-hydrogen compressor.

I had at last succeeded in separating soul from body, and secured it in the flask, but my suspicions were aroused one day when I noticed an odd smell of goat's milk, and before I was able to readjust the Hertz Oscillator which had obviously stopped working for a few moments, the catastrophe had occurred and my *anima pastoris* had irrevocably escaped.

I had immediate resort to the most powerful means of luring it back: I hung a pair of pink flannel knickers (Llama Brand) out on the window-sill, alongside an ivory backscratcher and a volume of poetry bound in cyanide-blue and embellished on the cover with golden knobs, but it was all in vain!

I had recourse to the laws of occult telenergy – again it was to no avail!

A distilled soul is hardly likely to allow itself to get caught! And now it's floating freely about in space, teaching the innocent souls of other planets the infernal secrets of female handicrafts: I found today that it had even managed *to crochet a new ring round Saturn*.

That really was the last straw. I thought things through, and cudgelled my brain for a solution until I came up with two possibilities: either to use deliberate provocation, as in the case of Scylla, or to act in an opposite sense, like Charybdis.

You are familiar with that brilliant statement by the great Johannes Müller: 'When the retina of the eye is stimulated by light, pressure, heat, electricity or any other irritation, the corresponding sensations are not specifically those of light, pressure, heat, electricity etc., but merely sensations of *sight*; and when the skin is illuminated, pressed, bombarded with sound or electrified, only *feeling* and its concomitants are generated.' This irrefutable law holds here too – for if you apply a stimulus to the clergywife's essential nucleus, no matter by what means, it *will start crocheting*; if however it is left undisturbed' - and here the Master's tones grew faint and hollow – '*it merely reproduces.*'

And with these words he sank back, lifeless.

Axel Wijkander clasped his hands together, deeply moved. 'Let us pray, brothers. He has passed on, on to the tranquil realm. May his soul rest in peace and joy for ever!'

THE AUTOMOBILE

'I don't suppose you remember me, Professor! Zimt is the name, Tarquin Zimt. I was a Maths and Physics student with you a few years ago.'

The Professor fiddled uncertainly with the visiting card, and in his embarrassment assumed an expression of recognition.

'And since my route was going to take me straight through Greifswald, I didn't want to miss the opportunity of paying you a visit.'

Some time went by in painful silence. 'Erm . . . didn't want to miss . . .'

The Professor, with a look of disapproval, allowed his eye to survey the figure of his leather-clad visitor. 'You must be a whaler?' he asked with gentle mockery, tapping the young man on his sleeve.

'No, no, I'm an automobilist; I am myself the proprietor of the famous marque: Zi . . .'

'An actor, then,' interrupted the Professor impatiently. But why did you study Maths and Physics? Changed direction, eh, my young friend? Changed direction! Well, well!'

'But not at all, Professor, by no means. Quite the contrary – just the opposite, as it were. I am a constructor of automobiles – motors – petrol motors – an engineer!'

'Ah, I understand: you assemble those fantasy images for the cinematograph. But you can hardly call that being an engineer.'

'No, no, I build automobiles – or horseless carriages, if you prefer. Our annual sales are already . . .'

'My dear Mr. Zimt, I can accept neither of these names, neither automobile nor horseless carriage, for to suppose that such a machine can move of itself – that must surely be the meaning of 'auto-mobile' – is out of the question. For the same reason, the expression 'horseless carriage' is equally meaningless'.

'What do you mean, cannot move of itself? In ten year's time, perhaps, we shall have no other means of transport. Factories are springing up everywhere, and just because there don't happen to be any automobiles in Greifswald, it doesn't . . .'

'You're a fantasist, young man: the ground is slipping away from under your feet. Have you taken up Spiritualism? It really is the most regrettable sign of the times to have to be continually putting up with the spectre of the *perpetuum mobile* raising its ugly head. As if the laws of Physics just didn't exist. Pitiful, it really is pitiful!

And to think that you, so recently my own student, could disown the clear and rational method of our science in favour of chasing after the stuffy, febrile fantasies of crude and thoughtless empiricism! Oh yes, city life these days may well have a debilitating effect on the intellectual capacity of our Youth, but it's still a mighty step to the mad idea – the absurd superstition – that you could actively propel a carriage using petrol engines; or so at least you want me to believe!' And the Professor polished furiously at his spectacles. Tarquin Zimt was at a complete loss.

'But for Heaven's sake, Professor! You're surely not trying to deny the existence of the motor-car? When there are already so many thousands actually on the road? When every month heralds a new make? Why, I have myself driven all the way here from Florence in my own automobile – a 50 h.p. 'Zimt', a vehicle I designed and constructed myself. Take a look out of the window, please, and you will see it outside your door. For Heaven's sake, I mean, for Heaven's sake!'

'*Omnia mea mecum porto*' as the Latin will have it, my young friend. I see no sufficient reason to look out of the window: why should I, after all, since my comprehensive mathematical understanding resides in me. Why should I place any reliance on the insecure ground of sense-perceptions?

Doesn't that simple formula which every young schoolboy knows –you can surely easily remember it too, from your own university days– tell me more – more than my own senses ever can? The formula:

$$M = \mu \int p \, d F y = 2 \mu r^2 1 \int_p^{\varphi^0} d\varphi^1$$

$$= 2 \pi \, Pr \frac{\sin \varphi^0}{\varphi^0 + \sin \varphi^0 \cos \varphi^0}$$

and so on! You see?'

'But that's all beside the point,' replied the engineer with some irritation, 'because I have myself driven in my own automobile from Florence to Greifswald, right up to your front door!'

'And even if the formula I've just quoted,' went on the professor unperturbed, 'probably isn't the most appropriate to apply to the so-called cylindrical pump, in as much as the increase in surface pressure proportionate to the reduction in the arc-radius of the bearing case does not produce an increase in the value of π and in so far as it is appropriate at all, reduces fuel consumption by a reduction in friction of $\varphi^0 \langle \frac{\pi}{2}$, there would still be a number of objections, any one of which would invalidate all possible suggestion . . .'

'But for Heaven's sake, Professor . . .'

'Pardon me! – all possible suggestion of any imaginable success in that direction in the most obvious and self-evident way. How can - let me put it in layman's terms, for example with respect to the mechanical limitations - how can the explosions of petrol vapour mixture in rapid succession in the cylinders a, b, c, d, thus causing a constantly rising and increasingly significant heat curve, with a consequent expansion and resulting pressure on the cylinder walls, until the metal of the piston seizes immovably in the cylinder, – how can this effect be obviated, except by the continuous and substantial application of a constant supply of quantities of fresh water, sufficient for effective cooling? And with respect to the inverse effect of weight on the power generation capacity of the motor, this again makes the result of the experiment crystal clear in a negative sense. Furthermore . . .'

'I have driven from Florence to Greifswald' interjected the other with dogged persistence.

'Furthermore, if on the basis of the formula:

$$P = \left(\frac{n}{30}\right)^2 r \left(\cos\varphi \pm \frac{r}{e}\cos 2\varphi\right)\left(G_1 + G_2\right)$$

$$+ \left(\frac{n}{30}\right)^2 r\, G_3 \cos\varphi$$

we consider that through vibration and other oscillations detrimental to steady motion in consequence of their own particular generation of inertial forces, resulting in the undesirable creation of movement in some parts of the machine, even if these are elastic, continual changes of shape are bound to occur, so that . . .'

'Even so, I have driven from Florence to Greifswald.'

' . . . changes of shape are bound to occur, so that . . .'

'But – I – really – have – dri-ven from Florence to Greifswald!'

The Professor glanced reprovingly at the speaker over the top of his spectacles.

'There would be nothing to stop me, on the basis of convincing mathematical formulae, from giving expression to my dubiety about your statement quite directly; but I will prefer, in the manner of the Ancient Greeks, to eschew any insult and instead merely emphasise, as Parmenides did before me, that it ill behoves the wise to ascribe any power of conviction to his own senses, let alone to those of a stranger.'

Tarquin Zimt reflected for a moment, and then reached into a pocket and pulled out some photographs, which he handed to the Professor in silence.

The latter cast no more than a glance at them before saying: 'Now, do you really think, my young friend, that a few photographic images of automobiles supposedly in movement are going to be able to bring the laws of mechanics into disrepute? I will remind you, just for the sake of the similarity of the circumstances, of the pictures of animistic phenomena produced by Crookes, Lombroso, Ochorowicz and Mendeleev! People know these days precisely how to doctor such photographs by all sorts of artificial means in order to disguise the true facts. What is more, was it not Heraclitus who demonstrated by the laws of logic that at every point in its flight, mathematically speaking, an arrow is actually motionless? Now, you see. More than that, in a figurative sense, your pictures cannot prove, with the best will in the world.'

At this point a sly thought gleamed in the engineer's eye, and with hypocritical expression, he replied: 'You will not, most honoured Professor, surely deny me, your most admiring former student, the request that you should at least look at my automobile, standing as it does outside your house?'

The professor nodded assent in condescending fashion, and they both made their way into the street.

A crowd of people had gathered around the vehicle.

Tarquin Zimt winked at his chauffeur: 'Ignaz! The professor would like to examine our automobil: show him the machine, please.'

The mechanic, thinking this was a matter of a sale, launched into a hymn of praise. 'Our 'Zimt' will do a hundred and fifty kilometres an hour, and on the whole journey here from Florence we have had not a single breakdown. We use . . .'

'Enough of that, my good fellow,' interposed the professor, with an embarrassed smile.

The chauffeur lifted the bonnet to reveal the engine and began to point out the various components.

'How now, Professor,' enquired Tarquin Zimt in a tone of suppressed derision, 'how do you reconcile the fact that many thousands of such vehicles are being built in the factories of Messrs Daimler, Benz, Dürrkopp, Opel, Brasier, Panhard, Fiat and so on, with your assertion that these machines cannot possibly work? Anyway, Ignaz, start the motor!'

'Reconcile? My young friend, I am merely an academic, and however interesting the solution to this question may be to a psychologist, I must confess it is of little moment to me to know why these factories should want to indulge in such an apparently fatuous occupation.'

The purring of the idling engine interrupted the professor's flow. The crowd of bystanders stepped back a pace.

Tarquin Zimt grinned. 'So you still don't believe that the vehicle will move, Professor? I need only pull this lever, the clutch will engage, and the automobile will speed away at a hundred and fifty kilometres per hour.'

The academic allowed himself a gentle smile. 'Oh, you young fanatics! Nothing of the kind can possibly occur. With the force of the explosion – supposing the clutch to be secure – cylinders a, b and d will on the contrary blow up. In all probability cylinder c will be untouched, according to the formula . . . now which formula is that? . . . the formula . . .'

'Let's go,' cried Zimt eagerly. 'Let her go, Ignaz!'

The chauffeur pulled the lever.

Bang! There was a loud, threefold explosion, and the engine stopped.

Uproar!

Ignaz jumps down. A long period ensues while he examines the engine. Behold! Cylinders one, two and four have blown up. Blown up so comprehensively that not even nitroglycerine inside them could have achieved such a result.

The professor is staring into the distance with a preoccupied expression, his lips repeating the phrase, 'wait a moment . . . according to the formula . . . the formula . . .'

Zimt grabs him by the arm and shakes him, almost crying with rage. 'It's impossible, unbelievable: nothing like it has ever occurred since the invention of the automobile! It's absolutely crazy, it's beyond reason! I shall wire at once for some spare cylinders. This won't do. You must convince yourself with your own eyes – you absolutely must!'

The professor pulls himself free with a gesture of irritation.

'Young man, this is going too far – you forget yourself. Do you honestly think I have any more time to waste on watching your childish experiments for a second time? Haven't you been convinced yet? Just thank your lucky stars that it didn't turn out any worse; machines are not things to be played about with. You see?'

And he hurries back indoors. As he reaches the threshold he turns once more, wags a finger in lofty disapproval and calls angrily:

'*Sunt pueri pueri pueri puerilia tractant.*'

THE WAXWORKS

'It was such a good idea of yours to send Melchior Kreuzer a wire: do you think he will do as we ask, Sinclair? If he took the first train' – Sebaldus glanced at his watch – 'he should be here any moment.'

Sinclair had stood up, and by way of reply was pointing out of the window.

They could see a tall, gaunt man hurrying up the street.

'Sometimes there are moments in your life when quite ordinary everyday events seem fearfully novel, don't you think, Sinclair? It's like waking up suddenly and then falling asleep again, and in that intervening heartbeat of time getting a glimpse of all kinds of ominous and mysterious events.'

Sinclair looked attentively at his friend: 'What are you getting at?'

'I suppose it's probably the waxworks that have upset me,' Sebaldus went on, 'I'm unspeakably nervous today. When I saw Melchior just now in the distance, and watched his figure getting bigger and bigger as he approached, I could feel some kind of perturbation, I don't know how to say it, but it was something uncanny, as if the distance could swallow up everything, no matter what: bodies, sounds, thoughts, fancies, events. Or conversely, as if we could see them tiny at first, then slowly getting bigger, everything, even non-material things, which don't have to move through space in the same way. – I don't think I'm using the right words here, but you know what I mean? Everything seems to obey the same law!'

His friend nodded thoughtfully.

'Yes, and there are some thoughts and happenings that come creeping up, as if there were an 'over there', like a hill or something that they can hide behind; and then they jump out right in front of you when they've grown to giant size.'

The door clicked open, and Dr. Kreuzer joined them at the bar.

'Melchior Kreuzer: Christian Sebaldus Obereit, Chemist', said Sinclair, introducing them.

'I can imagine why you sent me the wire,' said the new arrival. 'Lucretia's old trouble!? I couldn't help shuddering when I read Mohammed Daryashkoh's name in the paper. Have you discovered anything? Is it the same man?'

The tent housing the waxworks had been erected in the unpaved market-place, and the last reflections of dusk glinted pink from the hundred little angular mirrors that spelled out the ornamental words across the top of the canvas portico:

Mohammed Daryashkohs Oriental Panopticon
Presented by Mr. Congo-Brown

The canvas sides of the tent, brightly embellished with crudely painted scenes, swayed gently and billowed out like taut cheeks as the people inside moved about or leaned for a moment against the cloth.

Two wooden steps led up to the entrance, above which there stood, behind a glass panel, a lifesize wax image of a woman in a sequinned leotard.

Her pale face with its glass eyes rotated slowly, surveying the crowd below pressing around the tent, and looking from one to another before glancing to the side as if waiting for a covert signal from the dark-skinned Egyptian who presided over the cash desk. Then in a series of three jerky movements the head twisted completely backwards, before slowly and hesitantly unwinding again to return to its starting point, staring listlessly ahead. From time to time the figure suddenly twitched its arms and legs as if struck with a violent cramp, threw its head right back and bent over, till its forehead grazed its heels.

'It's that motor over there which drives the clockwork controlling these grotesque movements,' murmured Sinclair, pointing to the polished machine on the other side of the doorway rattling away to a four-stroke rhythm.

'Electrissiti, life si, all alife' pattered the Egyptian up above, handing them down a printed slip of paper.

'In half-hour, begin, si.'

'Do you think this fellow possibly knows where we can find Mohammed Daryashkoh?' asked Obereit.

But Melchior Kreuzer wasn't listening. He was engrossed in the leaflet, reading aloud those phrases that struck him most forcefully.

"The magnetic twins Vayu and Dhananjaya (with vocal accompaniment)': what's that? Did you see that yesterday?' he asked suddenly.

Sinclair replied in the negative. 'The living performers are only supposed to arrive today, and . . .' But Sebaldus Obereit interrupted him. 'You were personally acquainted with Thomas Charnoque, though, Dr. Kreuzer, Lucretia's husband?' 'Of course, we were friends for years.' 'And you never felt he might not take kindly to the child?' Dr. Kreuzer shook his head. 'I could see there was some mental illness slowly developing, but nobody could foresee the way it broke out so suddenly. He would torment poor Lucretia with such awful jealous scenes, and when we as his friends tried to show him how groundless his suspicions were, he would hardly listen. He was obsessed! Then, when the child came, we thought things would get better with him. And for a while they seemed to do so. But his mistrust had just sunk deeper, and one day we got the frightful news that he had suddenly gone mad, had stormed and shouted, and had then torn the baby out of its cradle and made off with him.

All enquiries proved fruitless. Someone thought he had seen him with Mohammed Daryashkoh at a railway station. And then a few years later news came, I think from Italy, that a foreigner called Thomas Charnoque, who had often been seen in the company of a small child and an Oriental gentleman, had been found hanged. But of Daryashkoh and the boy there was no trace. Since then every enquiry has come to nothing, so I can scarcely believe that the sign hanging up outside this tent has anything to do with that Asian. And then, what of that odd name Congo-Brown? I can't help thinking Thomas Charnoque must have mentioned it once at some time or other. Mohammed Daryashkoh was a Persian with an aristocratic background, too, with an unexampled breadth of knowledge – what would he be doing as the proprietor of a waxworks?'

'Perhaps Congo-Brown was a servant of his, who has misappropriated his master's name?' suggested Sinclair. 'Maybe. We shall have to follow the trail. But I'm still certain that the Asian encouraged Charnoque to make off with the child – indeed, that he put him up to it.

He hated Lucretia absolutely. To judge by something she said once, it seems to me that he was continually pestering her with proposals, even though she found him repulsive.

But there must be some other deeper mystery to explain Daryashkoh's passion for revenge.

There's nothing more to be got out of Lucretia, and she almost passes out with emotion if you make even an incidental reference to the affair.

All in all, Daryashkoh was an evil genius behind this family. Thomas Charnoque was completely under his thumb; he often told us he thought the Persian was the only man alive to have penetrated the mysteries of some kind of secret preadamite skill, which actually enabled him to take a human being apart, and separate out the various living organs, for his own quite inexplicable purposes.

Of course, we thought Thomas was making it all up, and that Daryashkoh was just a malicious swindler, yet there was never any proof or evidence . . . But the show's about to start. Isn't that the Egyptian lighting the lamps round the tent?'

'Fatima, Pearl of the Orient' had played her piece, and the spectators were walking to and fro or squinting through the peepholes cut in the red cloth walls at a crudely painted panorama of the siege of Delhi.

Others were standing in silent contemplation of a glass coffin, in which lay the body of a dying Turk, breathing heavily, his bare chest displaying the seared and livid-edged wound inflicted by the impact of a cannon-ball. As the wax figure opened its leaden eyes the gentle whirring of machinery could be heard from the casket, and the bystanders would put their ear to the glass, the better to hear the sound.

The motor at the entrance pumped away, driving some kind of musical organ. It was playing a tune with a stumbling, breathless beat, loud and muffled at the same time, the notes sounding strange and sodden, as if the thing was being played under water.

The air in the tent was heavy with the smell of wax and smoky oil-lamps.

'No. 311: Obeah-Wanga voodoo skulls' Sinclair read from his leaflet as they both gazed at three severed heads arranged in a cabinet set against the wall in a corner, incredibly lifelike, with mouths gaping and eyes staring with horrific expressions.

'Do you know, those are not wax at all – they're genuine!' said Obereit with astonishment, pulling a magnifying glass from his pocket. 'But I just don't understand how it's been done. It's extraordinary, the whole of the cut surface of the neck has been covered over with silk – or perhaps it has grown over. And I can't see any joins! It just looks exactly as though they have grown like pumpkins, and have never sat on human shoulders at all. If only we could just lift the glass lid a little!'

'All wax, si, life wax, si – real dead head too dear, and smell – phoo,' said the Egyptian, suddenly materialising behind them. He had sidled up to them without their noticing: his face twitched, as if he were trying to suppress a mad laugh.

The two visitors exchanged a startled glance. 'Let's hope the old gyppo heard nothing – we were just talking about Daryashkoh,' said Sinclair after a while.

'Do you think Dr. Kreuzer will manage to get anything

out of Fatima? If the worst comes to the worst we shall have to invite her round one evening to share a bottle of wine. He's still standing out there talking to her.'

The music stopped abruptly, someone sounded a gong and a piercing female voice penetrated through the curtain: 'Vayu and Dhananjaya, magnetic twins, 8 years old. The greatest marvel in the world. They will sssing!'

The crowd pressed towards the stage at the back of the tent.

Dr. Kreuzer had re-entered the tent: he grasped Sinclair's arm. 'I've got an address,' he whispered. 'The Persian is living in Paris under an assumed name. Here it is.'

And he surreptitiously displayed a scrap of paper to the two friends. 'We must take the next train to Paris!'

'Vayu and Dhananjaya. They will sssing!' screeched the voice once more.

The curtain drew aside, and there lurched onto the stage a grotesque and gruesome figure dressed as a page and carrying a bundle under one arm.

The re-animated corpse of a drowned man, with long blond hair and dressed in scraps of multicoloured velvet.

A ripple of revulsion spread through the crowd.

The thing was the size of an adult, but it had the features of a child. Its face, arms and legs, its whole body indeed, even down to the fingers, were inexplicably swollen and bloated.

It was inflated, like a thin rubber balloon. The skin on the lips and hands were drained of colour, almost translucent, as if they were full of air or water, and the eyes looked dead, without a flicker of comprehension.

It stared helplessly about.

'Vayu, se greater brosair,' explained the hidden female voice with its peculiar accent; and from behind the curtain, fiddle in hand, a woman appeared in the guise of an animal-tamer, and wearing high red Polish boots trimmed with fur.

'Vayu' she said again, indicating the inflated child with her fiddle-bow. Then she opened a small book she was carrying and read out aloud:

'Sese two male childs are now eight year old, and se great marvel. Sey join only by se navel cord, which iss tree ell long and altogeser transparent. If one iss cut off, se osair must die. It iss astonishment to all scientists. Vayu, he iss far above his age. Developed. But behind in mind, while Dhananjaya, he iss so very clevair, but so very small. Like a baby. For he iss born wiss no skin, and grows not. He must be kept in animal bubble, in warm water. Se parents are not ever known. It iss se greatest sport of nature.'

She signed to Vayu, who with great hesitation unwrapped the bundle on his arm.

A head the size of a fist was revealed, with great piercing eyes.

A face, a blue-veined baby face, yet so ancient a mien and with an expression so menacingly twisted with hate, evil and full of such indescribable vileness that the spectators involuntarily shrank back.

'M – My brother D – D -Dhananjaya,' stammered the inflated creature staring at the public again uncomprehendingly.

'Take me out – I think I'm going to faint. God almighty!' whispered Melchior Kreuzer. They led him stumbling slowly, half unconscious, towards the exit, and past the sly and watchful gaze of the Egyptian.

The woman had picked up her fiddle, and they heard her strike up a song to accompany the strangled voice of the overblown child;

> 'Oh once I had a comrade true
> You'll never find a better.'

And the infant, incapable of articulating the words properly, shrilled along, echoing in piercing tones no more than the mere vowel sounds:

> *'Owahai haha howa wu*
> *iou ea ai a ea.'*

Dr. Kreuzer hung heavily on Sinclair's arm, gulping in the fresh air.

The sound of applause drifted out of the tent.

'It's Charnoques face! What a fearful similarity,' groaned Melchior Kreuzer. 'But how – I don't understand. Everything was spinning in front of my eyes, I was sure I was going to faint. Sebaldus, please, fetch a cab. I've got to tell the authorities. Something's got to be done. You, both of you, get off to Paris – Mohammed Daryashkoh – you must have him arrested at once.'

The two friends were sitting once more looking out of the window of the secluded cafe at Melchior Kreuzer as he hurried up the street.

'Just as it was before,' said Sinclair. 'Fate is so miserly with her scenarios!'

They heard the door close with a click. Dr. Kreuzer entered, and they shook hands.

'You really do owe us a long report,' said Sebaldus Obereit eventually, after Sinclair had detailed how they had spent fully two fruitless months in Paris in pursuit of the Persian. 'You sent us so little information.'

'I nearly lost the ability to write; speaking too, nearly,' apologised Kreuzer.

'I feel I have grown so old since then. When you're continually presented with new puzzles, you get worn down faster than you think. Most people can't possibly imagine what it means for those who always have to carry some eternally insoluble riddle about in their minds. And then, to have to watch poor Lucretia's agonies every day!

It wasn't long ago that she died – I wrote you that – of grief and despair.

Congo-Brown escaped from the prison where he was waiting to be questioned, and that was the end of the last source from which we might have got at the truth.

I'll tell you everything in detail sometime later, when the immediacy of it all has receded. It's all too close just yet.'

'But aren't there any clues at all?' asked Sinclair.

'It was a bleak picture I uncovered. Things our medical department could not or would not credit. Black superstition, tissues of lies, hysterical self-deceit they insisted on calling it, and yet there was so much that was frighteningly obvious.

I had everyone arrested at once. Congo-Brown admitted that the twins, indeed the whole Panopticon for that matter – had been given to him by Daryashkoh in return for earlier services rendered, and that Vayu and Dhananjaya were an artificially created double figure, which the Persian had put together out of the elements of a single child (Thomas Charnoque's own son), without interrupting its vital function. He had simply teased out a number of magnetic currents of a kind which exist in every one of us and which can be individually picked out by means of certain secret processes, and then, with the aid of some organic additives, created two quite different consciousnesses possessing quite different characteristics.

Altogether, Daryashkoh was an expert in the most abstruse arts. Even the three Obeah-Wanga skulls were no more than the remains of other experiments, which had been previously kept alive for some time. It was all confirmed by Fatima, Congo-Brown's *inamorata*, and everyone else, who were themselves all quite innocent.

Fatima further deposed that Congo-Brown was an epileptic who during certain phases of the moon would be seized with a strange state of mind in which he imagined he was Mohammed Darayaskoh himself. In this condition his pulse would cease, his breathing would be arrested and his features undergo an alteration, such that you would imagine you had Daryashkoh himself (who had in the past often been seen about in Paris) right in front of you.

Furthermore, he would under these circumstances emanate such an undeniable magnetic force that, without having to issue any sort of order, he could induce anyone to imitate every movement or forced gesture that he himself proposed. It was as if people were struck by

St. Vitus' dance – irresistible. He possessed an unparalleled suppleness, and could for example produce every sort of dervish-movement by means of which he could generate the most enigmatic phenomena and shifts of consciousness (the Persian had personally taught him these) – gestures so elaborate that no contortionist in the world could follow them.

In the course of their travels from place to place with the waxworks Congo-Brown had occasionally attempted to use this mesmeric power to force children to mirror these distortions. Most of them had shattered their spines. The rest had been so affected in the mind that they had been reduced to imbecility. Our doctors naturally shook their heads at Fatima's assertions, but subsequent events must have given them pause for thought. Congo-Brown in fact absconded from the chambers where he was being examined through a side-room, and the magistrate reported that just as he was about to start an interrogation the fellow had suddenly stared at him and waved his arms about in an odd fashion. The magistrate had felt a sudden uncertainty and had attempted to ring for assistance, but he had been struck by a paralytic attack, his tongue had somehow twisted round in a way he could not now recall (the whole fit must have begun with this feeling in his mouth) and he had then passed out.'

'Couldn't they find out anything about how Mohammed Daryashkoh had made this double creature without actually killing the child?' interrupted Sebaldus. Dr. Kreutzer shook his head. 'No. I thought a lot about what Thomas Charnoque had told me once, though. A human life is quite different from what we imagine, he used to say; it is made up from a number of magnetic currents that circulate partly within and partly outside the body; and our scientists are wrong to assert that someone who has had his skin removed is bound to die for lack of oxygen. The element that the skin draws from the atmosphere is something quite different from oxygen. Furthermore, the skin doesn't really absorb this fluid – it is only a kind of grid serving to enable the current to cover the surface – rather like a piece of wire netting which, dipped in soapy water, enables the bubbles to spread across all its spaces. Even people's spiritual character, he said, was shaped by the dominance of this or that current, so that an excess of one particular one could produce a character of such extraordinary depravity that it exceeded our comprehension.'

Melchior fell silent for a moment, lost in his own thoughts.

'And when I think of what horrific properties that dwarf Dhananjaya possessed, which kept his life perpetually renewed, I can only see the awful confirmation of that theory.'

'You speak as if the twins were dead. Have they died?' asked Sinclair with surprise.

'A few days ago. And it is as well that they did. The fluid that one of them spent most of his day in dried out, and nobody knew its composition.'

Melchior Kreuzer stared into space and shuddered. 'There were things so awful – so indescribably horrible – it's a blessing Lucretia never found out; that at least was spared her! Just to see that frightful double creature was enough to unhinge her! It was just as if her maternal feelings had been torn in half.

Just let me forget all that for today. The thought of Vayu and Dhananjaya – it still makes my head reel.' He sat a while in contemplation, then jumped up suddenly, exclaiming 'Pour me some wine – I don't want to think about it any more. Let's change the subject – Music, anything, just to dream up some different thoughts! Music!

And he stumbled across to a gleaming juke-box standing against the wall, and tossed a coin into the slot.

Clink. The money fell audibly inside and the machine ground into motion.

Three odd notes sounded, then a moment later the tune blared across the room:

> 'Oh, once I had a comrade true
> You'll never find a better'.

FEVER

Alchemist: who art thou, dim shade
  in the glass here? I bid thee speak.
The Matter in the Retort: Ater corvus sum.

Once upon a time there was a man who was so tired of the
world that he decided to stay in bed. Every time he woke
up he turned over on to the other side, so that he always
managed to sleep on a little longer.

But one day this plan wouldn't work any more: it just
would not, he could not go on. And he lay there in bed,
quite still, for fear that if he changed his position he would
shiver.

He had to look out through the window from his
pillow, and just at the moment when his sleep was quite at
an end, the sun was setting.

A broad, golden-yellow wound gaped across the sky
beneath a dark, heady mass of cloud.

'It certainly won't do to get up, just at such a fateful
moment,' said the man, his teeth chattering - and he was
even more afraid than before that he might shiver – 'even
for someone who is not so tired of the world as I am.' And
he stared with melancholy gaze into the yellow evening, its
glowing rim huddled beneath the skirt of fog. One black
cloud had drifted away from the rest, shaped like a curving
wing, feathers visible at the edge.

And from out of her burrow there crept into the man's
head, with the fluffy outlines of a fur muff, the recollection
of a dream. A dream of a raven, brooding upon a heart.

And all through his long sleep he had been wrestling
with this dream – of that the man was now quite certain.

'I must discover whose this wing is,' he said, and climbed
out of bed in his nightshirt, down the stairs, and out into
the street; and he went, on and on, always in the direction
of the sunset.

But the people he met whispered: 'pst, pst, pst, hush, hush, he's dreaming it all.'

Only Vrieslander, baker of consecrated wafers by formal appointment, thought himself to be in a position to make a joke. He stood in the man's path, pursed his lips and made round eyes like a fish. His wispy tailor's beard seemed even more phantasmal than usual, and with his bony arms and fingers he cut a splayed, and madly twisted pose, and crooked his legs most strangely. 'Psst psst, gently, do you hear?' he whispered venomously; 'my name is Giggle, you know, Gig . . .' and he suddenly jerked his sharp knee up into his chest, and pulled his mouth wide open, while his cheeks drained to a leaden pallor, as if he had been over-taken in the midst of his pirouette by Death.

The man in his nightshirt felt the hair on his head stand on end for horror, and he ran on, out of the town, across meadows and stubble fields, always towards the sunset, always with his feet bare.

From time to time his foot slipped on a frog.

Only when it was night, long after the burning slit in the sky had closed again, did he reach the long white wall, behind which the cloudy wing had vanished.

He sat down on a little hill. 'Here I am then, in the burial ground,' he said to himself, and looked about him. 'Well, now, this may turn out to be awful nonsense. But I must find out who the wing belongs to!'

As the night wore on it grew gradually lighter, and the moon crept slowly above the wall. A kind of dawning astonishment spread across the sky.

As the moonlight's harsh illumination swept across the ground flocks of blue-black birds flew up out of the ground behind the gravestones, slipping up behind, from the side turned away from the light, to rest silently on the whitewashed wall.

Then for a space a corpse-like immobility was cast over all.

'That is the dark wood in the distance of course, rising out of the mists, and the round head in the middle is the hill with its crown of trees,' dreamed the man in the nightshirt. But when he looked more closely it was a monstrous raven, perched with pinions outstretched on the wall over there.

'Ah, the wing –' thought the man, pleased with himself, 'the wing . . .' And the bird, inflated with pride, boasted: 'I am the raven who broods on hearts. When someone breaks a heart it is brought straight away to me.' And it flapped down from the wall and came to rest perched on a stone of marble, and the wind of the beat of its wings had the odour of withered flowers.

But under the marble stone lay one who had but today come to join his family.

The man in his nightshirt spelled out a name, and was curious to know what kind of a bird would hatch from this shattered heart; for the newly deceased had been a well-known philanthropist, had devoted his whole life to enlightenment, had done and said nothing but good, had cleansed the Bible and had been the author of elevating tracts. His eyes, simple and without guile, like saucer-mirrors, had radiated goodwill in life, and now too, in golden letters upon his grave was written:

> Loyalty and Honesty be ever thine
> Unto your cool grave,
> And step not aside one whit
> From the path of righteousness.

The man in the nightshirt watched with rapt attention. A gentle crackling rose up out of the grave, as the young chick eased itself from its heart's shell – and then it fluttered off with a croak, a pitch-black shadow flitting up to join the others along the wall.

'But that was really to be expected, was it not? Or were you in your innocence perhaps expecting a partridge?' mocked the raven.

'There is something white about it, even so,' said the man doggedly, by which he meant one light, bright feather,

148

which clearly stood out. The raven laughed. 'That goose-down? That's just stuck on. It's come out of the feather pillow the man always slept on!' And it flew on from grave to grave, settling for a while here and there, and everywhere the fledglings came fluttering, sable-black from the earth.

'Black? Are they all, all black?' asked the man after a while, sick at heart.

'Black. All, all black!' snarled the raven in reply.

And the man in his nightshirt was sorry that he had not stayed in his bed.

And as he looked up at the sky, the stars were full of tears, blinking.

Only the moon stared wide-eyed, uncomprehending.

But suddenly there sat, quite still on a cross, another raven, and it was shining snowy white. And it seemed as if all the glimmer of the light came from it. The man only saw it because he happened to turn his head that way. And on the cross the inscription named one who had been an idler his whole life long.

The man in the nightshirt had known him well. And he pondered long.

'What deed was it that made his heart so white, then?' he asked at last.

But the black raven had grown ill-tempered, and was repeatedly trying to jump over its own shadow.

'What deed, what deed, what deed?' The man went on, importunate. Then the raven burst out in anger: 'Do you think it is *deeds* that can make it white? You . . . you . . . *cannot* even *do* a deed! I should as easily jump over my own shadow. That jumping jack there, rotting to pieces on the tiny grave – do you see it? – Once it belonged to the child buried beneath. And for a long time that decaying toy too thought he was a great fellow in the world. Because he couldn't see the strings he was hanging by, and would not believe it was a child who played with him. And you – you? What do you think will happen to *you* when the – 'Child' abandons you for another toy? You'll be laid out and you'll cr . . .'

The raven glanced slyly across at the wall – 'and you'll cr . . .' 'Croak!' went the raven-flock, overjoyed at the chance to join it.

And the man in the nightshirt was afraid, quite inordinately so.

'So what else made his heart so white? Listen to me, what else made his heart so white?' he asked.

The raven shifted uneasily from one foot to the other. 'It must have been the yearning. Yearning for something hidden, that I do not know and have never found on earth. We all saw his yearning grow like fire, and understood it not. It burned up his blood, and eventually it burned up his brain: we understood it not.'

The man in the nightshirt grasped the idea ice-cold: The Light Shineth In Darkness, And The Darkness Comprehended It Not.

'Yes, we did not comprehend,' continued the raven, 'but one of the gigantic, gleaming birds, that have hovered eternally unmoving in space since the beginning of time, spied the glowing spark and stooped down. Like white-hot fire. And He has brooded on that man's heart, night after night.

And vivid images now began to crowd in on the vision of the man in his nightshirt. Images which had never quite been able to die away from his memory – events in the fortune of the idler, that were passed among the people from mouth to mouth: he saw that man standing under the gallows – the hangman drawing the linen mask down over his face – the spring that was supposed to tilt the board under the feet of the poor sinner failing to operate; – they took him away and put the board straight. And once more the hangman reached for the linen mask; once more the spring would not work. And after a month, when the man again stood there, the linen mask across his eyes, once more – the spring broke in two.

But the judges – the judges in exasperation ground their teeth and cursed – cursed the carpenter, who had made the scaffold so badly.

★

Then the vision faded.

'And what became of him?' asked the man in the nightshirt, full of horror.

'I consumed his flesh, and his bones; and the earth has been diminished by the measure of his corpse,' said the white raven.

'Yes, yes,' whispered the black. 'His coffin is empty, he cheated the grave.'

All this the man heard, and his hair stood on end; he tore at the shirt on his breast and ran to the white bird perched on the cross, crying: 'Hatch out my heart, hatch out my heart! My heart too is full of longing!'

But it was the *black* raven that threw him to the ground with its pinions and settled heavily upon him. The air was filled with the odour of decaying flowers.

'Make no mistake, Cousin, it is greed, not longing, that slumbers in your heart! Yes, many would gladly try it before they cr . . .' and he glanced slyly across at the wall: 'before they cr . . .!'

'Roak!' went the raven assembly along the wall, delighted to be given their turn again.

The heat of his body was strange and agitating, like fever, he felt; and then his consciousness fluttered away in dissolution.

When he awoke from a long sleep the moon stood high in the sky, and was staring him in the face. Its brilliance had drunk up the shadows, and struck down on the stones from all sides.

The black ravens had gone.

But the man could still hear their spiteful croak in his ears, and with an unquiet mind he clambered over the wall and into his bed.

The doctor was there already in his black coat. He took the man's pulse, closed his eyes behind his gold-rimmed spectacles and babbled to himself long and inaudibly with a tremor of his lower lip. Then with a flourish he fetched out his notebook and wrote out a prescription:

Rp:

Cort. chin. reg. rud.tus 3β

coque c. suff. quant. vini rubri, per horam . j

ad colat 3viij

cum hac inf. herb. abs . . . 3j

    postea solve

acet. lix 3j

    tunc adde

syr. cort. aur 3β

    M. d. ad

    vitr. s.

One tablespoon 3 times daily

And when he had finished he stepped with a consecratory gesture to the door, turned back once again and said mysteriously, one finger raised with a dignified air:

'*Contra* the fever, *contra* the fever'.

WHAT'S THE USE OF WHITE DOG SHIT?

'Stand up, for King and Country'

Not many people know that it's good for anything.

But there's no doubt at all that it serves some special purpose.

When I leave the house first thing in the morning, just before the postman arrives and shoves a whole load of paper through the letterbox (I've rigged it up with a proper flushing system, by the way), I always stop in the garden for a moment and say out loud: 'Ksss, Ksss'.

And at once a most peculiar phenomenon takes place. A kind of wheezing cough can be heard from the dry leaves; a croaking and rustling, spitting sound. Two fiery eyes light up about a foot from the ground and then something black with a bald swelling on its neck comes hurtling out of the bushes at me, snapping madly at my trouser-creases.

What species of animal it belongs to I haven't yet succeeded in finding out.

It spends the morning crouching curled up under an elder bush: that at least I have managed to establish.

The maid swears the thing can sometimes be seen wearing a blue blanket lined with red and ornamented in the far corner with a crown. In spite of the closest observation I haven't been able to confirm this: it almost seems as if each person's retina responds to it in a different way.

Now, what this thing with the bald excrescence may be: whether, if we are to judge by the crown, it is the restless shade of the last degenerate scion of an extinct dynasty, taking on form under the influence of certain astrological constellations, or whether it is instead a single citizen of the animal kingdom – whatever it is, it does partake of a spectral quality, which continually causes me to doubt its corporeality.

I feel clearly it's as old as the hills, and I don't doubt it finds it easy enough to remember the battle of Cannae. There's a haze of history wafting about it.

But in spite of its antiquity there is no purity in it; the hatred of an entire world is able to find room in its heart.

It has never yet managed to get a good hold on my trouser-creases. This too would be evidence that it is no more than a reflection from another sphere. Something imponderable, invisible, seems to force it to turn away at the very last fraction of a moment, although it never tires of making the attempt, and is continually prepared to try again.

As suddenly as the phenomenon appears, so it vanishes. Then all at once, without any warning, a shrill voice in the sky shrieks: 'Ah-meee! Ah – meee!'

Quite clearly: 'Ah – meee!'

Now there's nothing particularly marvellous about that. The old Jews heard a voice from Heaven like that often enough; why shouldn't it happen to me in Columbus Lane?

On this thing with the blister however it has a quite devastating effect.

With a jerk the phantom tears itself away from me, scrabbles its way through the garden gate and around the corner where it instantly dematerialises!

On reflection, this word 'Ah-meee' seems to me to be one of those accursedly sonorous formulae such as you find referred to in the Lamrim of Tson-ka-pa, those terrible Tibetan books of magic, and which, when properly pronounced, are capable of raising in the causal realm astral whirlwinds of such power that even inside our protective material bodies we can become fearfully aware of the last eddies of these catastrophes as they become manifested in the form of mysteriously inexplicable happenings.

I have often chanted these strange syllables to myself: 'Ah-meee!' Hesitantly at first, but then more boldly, but there has never been any change visible in my material surroundings. I have obviously put the wrong stress on them. Or is their effectiveness dependent on a presumption of strict asceticism in the chanter?

The dematerialisation of this thing, which I witness every morning, is by no means the end of the sequence of events.

No sooner has the voice from above died away than a disabled soldier comes into my garden, and makes straight for the elder bush.

I never trust mere appearance – one's senses offer such an insecure guarantee of abstract perception – but the invalid is certainly genuine. I have had him photographed.

With an iron hook the old warrior lifts up a few bleached looking objects from the ground [*author's note:* without doubt they are white dog-turds] and transfers them with a triumphant flourish to a sack half full of similar items, which he carries at his right side, to balance the array of campaign medals pinned to his left. There is something diabolical about the way in which these pale objects are always to be found at the same spot – the very one that has just been vacated by the blistered Thing.

There is indubitably some kind of ghostly connection. If it were a case of any poor fellow being responsible for picking up these pallid substances, the matter would hardly be worth noticing. One would naturally think they had no more than a slight value, and could claim no more than a subsidiary role in nature's housekeeping. But here?

To have old soldiers collecting them?

Does not the fatherland with its bountiful hands heap honour and riches upon such people, in consciousness of our gratitude for their blood which was shed, and limbs which were shattered, in sacrifice for us?

What are they doing chasing after waste matter?

There's a double bottom to the case here!

These bleached objects must have some kind of special status. I realised this a good twelve months ago. But when one morning I read in the paper that they had found an old veteran of the Italian Campaign dead in his room, with nothing to his name but an iron poker and a sack of white dog excrement, I was overcome with a kind of fear, an awful need, to investigate the riddle as far as was remotely possible.

Of course there are plenty of doom-merchants who would say that disabled soldiers are poor. Their evil intention however is only too obvious. It's clear after all, that if the Fatherland were really not to give them support, then the Emperor himself would gladly step in. For in truth, a spirit of sacrifice for the Fatherland does not go unrewarded: our 'true' poets have always advocated such a stance.

Yet another old soldier, and yet another sack of a certain sort! And what had become of all his accumulated wealth, eh? He must have thought very little of it, I felt – 'What do I care about that, so long as I have the sack,' he must have said to himself.

And I remembered the Tale of the Dervish in the Arabian Nights, who forced his way into the Treasure House, only to leave all the jewels lying there untouched, taking with him only a little box of ointment which when applied to a man's eyes had the magic property of conferring absolute power on him.

Colossal value – the key to unheard-of pleasures must reside, I concluded, in these pale objects, if it were precisely these capricious veteran soldiers, indulged as heroes at every turn by a grateful public, who were prepared to ignore all the hardships of inclement weather, and to search round, leaving no stone unturned, to gain possession of them.

I rushed off straight away to the police. The iron poker was still there but the sack – the sack had vanished! And nobody knew what had become of it. Well now!

Someone or other must evidently have risked everything to get hold of it! And to have snatched it from the very jaws of the police at the last minute, with such unimaginable boldness!

'And what is the use of white dog dirt?' I asked myself. 'What *is* the use?'

I looked up the encyclopedia under D for dirt, under W for white, under S, under E – nothing.

To try to find the whereabouts of my old soldier would have been absurd. He least of all would have been prepared to betray his secret to me.

So I wrote to the Ministry of Education.

I received no reply.

I went to a presentation given by a well-known name in the entertainment world, where the audience wrote questions on little cards for him to answer. I added mine, but when he came to it he tore it up and walked out indignantly.

At the town hall I couldn't find the right office, and they wouldn't let me in to see the mayor.

'It's stuck on the ceilings of public rooms in government buildings as ornamentation,' suggested a cynic in a mocking tone. 'That's why they call it 'stucco'.'

'It is pathos among equals, it is an end in itself,' mused the poet Peter Altenberg.

An eminent academic on the other hand icily dismissed the whole thing, adding the stern advice: 'In polite company such things do not pass one's lips; they are in any case a sign of serious digestive problems, and they *serve* (and here his eyes flashed a rebuke) they *serve* as a warning to the well-to-do layman always to follow the advice of a competent medical professional in questions concerning the conduct of his life.'

By contrast, a workman whom I consulted said nothing at all, but gave me a box on the ear instead.

I followed other lines of enquiry. I accosted people in the street who had a furtive look to them, and asked them the question straight out, hoping to take them by surprise. Short, clear and to the point.

They took a step backwards in surprise and ran off, with every indication of fright!

So I decided to delve into the depths of the mystery all by myself, and to do some chemical experiments of my own, as well as to go hunting for the things on my own account.

But as if some dark power was making fun of me, the very spot under my elder tree stayed empty day after day and, strange to relate, the thing with the excrescence on its neck seemed to have disappeared.

I can't even think about it without a shudder.

I spent a whole week searching along deserted walls. I left no monument unvisited. All to no purpose!

And when at last Lady Luck smiled at me and I had laid hands on some of the precious stuff and placed it securely in a phial, a dreadful fear suddenly overcame me. What if I were to faint suddenly now, or to be seized with apoplexy? They would find the stuff on me, they would say, 'he had a bad soul, he was altogether perverse, the dirty pig'. And that would destroy my family's peace of mind for ever! And those army officers to whom I am allied by unbreakable bonds of the deepest fellow-feeling would turn their noses up, saying: 'I knew it all along: he was altogether a thoroughly rum fellow!

And the evangelical boys' club would fold their hands together and dance a Protestant Enlightenment fandango on my grave.

So I threw the phial away.

The next thing I did was to immerse myself in the study of the history of secret societies. There can't be a single fraternity left that I haven't joined, and if I were to go through all the profoundly meaningful secret signs and emergency signals that I learned one after the other, I'd be carted off to the asylum for sure, suspected of having contracted St. Vitus' dance.

But I'm not going to give up.

I must find out what function 'it' has.

Somewhere, every fibre of my being tells me, there is a fearsome Order, a silent assembly of men, for whom bolts and bars are as nothing, who are immune from the arrows of fortune and who have the world tamed in leading-strings. All power on earth is theirs, and they use it in order to engage unpunished in the most horrific orgies!

What else were the mediaeval Stercatorists, who always

boasted that they were the only ones among all the alchemists to possess the true 'materia', than adherents of this sect?

The old forgotten Ancient Order of Pugs, for instance – what other purpose can it have had?

And the grasp of the 'Brotherhood' reaches right into our own days!

Who is their Master? Where is the centre of their activities?

The sinister Ohlendorff, Hamburg's uncrowned guano-king must have been their last Grandmaster, I suppose, but who is it today?

What a mystery these veterans are!

Treasure upon treasure is piling up, raked together with their iron claws – and then, woe betide us!

I look into the future with great trepidation. Days pass, but nobody offers me a solution to my question : what use, what use is 'it' actually?

And dawn cracks open, the cock crows in apprehension of the tardy day, and there I lie, unable to sleep, while outside under the elder tree the phantom with its swollen neck is perhaps already going about its business.

In a half-daze I can visualize regiments of old soldiers hung about with medals striding onward to the Blocksberg. And I toss and turn in torment, groaning and sighing: What, oh what is the use of white dog shit?!

Author's postscript:

I refuse to accept explanations sent to me by members of the public of the sort: 'This mysterious material is used in the tanning process, to dress gloves.'

HUMMING IN THE EARS

In the old city of Prague, in the district called the Kleinseite, there stands an old house that has always been inhabited by discontented people. Everyone who enters it is struck by an excruciatingly uncomfortable sensation – a gloomy thing, buried up to its belly in the ground.

There is an iron trapdoor in the cellar. If you lift it up you can see a dark and narrow shaft descending coldly into the earth, its walls oozing with moisture. Many people have in the past let down torches tied on a line. Right down into the darkness, the light becoming weaker and smokier, until it goes out altogether, and the people have said:

There is no more air.

So nobody knows where the shaft goes.

But he who has eyes to see can see without light, even in the darkness, when others are asleep.

When people lie open to the night, and consciousness faints, then the soul of greed abandons the regular beat of the heart – it looks greenish in the haze, it takes on loose and shapeless forms, and is hideous, for there is no love in the hearts of men.

Exhausted by their daily labour, which they call their duty, they seek a renewal of strength in sleep, in order to destroy their brothers' fortune or to plan new murders to perpetrate in the coming sunlit hours.

And they sleep and snore.

It is then that the phantoms of greed slip lightly through the joints of doors and walls out into the open, into the attentive night; and slumbering beasts whimper and wince as they sense the presence of their executioners.

They slither and slide sidling into the gloomy old house, and down to the musty cellar with its iron trap. The metal weighs as nothing as the souls' hands slip round it. The shaft yawns wider deep below, and there the shadows gather.

They make no sign to each other, neither greeting nor question. There is nothing that the one might need to know from another.

In the middle of this space a grey whetstone disk spins dizzily, whirring at a prodigious rate. Thousands of years ago, long before Prague was built, it was tempered in the fire of hatred by the epitome of evil.

Against its whirling rim the phantoms sharpen their claws of greed, claws that have been scratched blunt on the daylight men. Sparks fly from these onyx claws of lust and from the steely spurs of rapaciousness.

They all, all are thus made razor-sharp once more, for the Prince of Evil has need of ever-renewed wounds.

If the man in his sleep wants to stretch his fingers, his phantom must return to its shell: for the claws must stay curled just so, that the hands cannot be clasped in prayer.

Satan's whetstone whirls on, unceasingly, day and night.

If you stop your ears, you can hear it, humming away inside you.

BAL MACABRE

Lord Hopeless had invited me to join him at his table, and he introduced me to the other gentlemen.

It was well past midnight, and I didn't catch most of the names.

I knew Dr. Trembler already.

'It's a shame, you're always on your own,' he said, as he shook me by the hand, 'why do you always sit alone?'

I know that we had not drunk all that much, and yet we had that slight, barely perceptible sense of intoxication where words seem to float in from a distance, that is characteristic of the small hours when one is bathed in a heady mixture of cigarette smoke, feminine laughter and inconsequential music.

Are you surprised that an atmosphere such as this, made up in equal measure of gipsy melodies, cake-walk and champagne should give rise to a conversation about the occult? Lord Hopeless was talking.

About a brotherhood of people – or rather, of the dead or seeming-dead, that in all seriousness really does exist. People of the most respectable sort, who are known by the living to have died long since, who even have gravestones and tombs with their names and dates of death carved on them, but who actually survive instead lying year after year in a state of suspended animation concealed in some antiquated property in the town, hidden in a drawer, without sensation and secure from decay, and watched over by a crookbacked ministrant in buckled shoes and powdered wig who goes by the name (if I heard right) of Spotted Aaron. On certain nights a dull, phosphorescent glow appears about their lips, an indication to the old cripple that it is time to engage in a certain abstruse manipulation of the cervical vertebrae of these apparent corpses. So he said.

This operation completed, their souls could float unhindered, free of the body for a space, to give themselves up to all the vice of the city with an urgency and intensity unthinkable even for the most depraved.

One feature was the way in which these vampires would fasten themselves like ticks to the living as they stumbled from one iniquity to the next, stealing and drawing sustenance from the nervous stimulation of the crowd. This club (it bore the curious name Amanita) even held meetings, with rules and statutes and strict requirements for the admission of new members. Yet over all there lay an impenetrable veil of secrecy.

I couldn't hear the final words of Lord Hopeless' disquisition, as they were drowned out by the band playing the latest popular hit:

'Oh, oh Sue,
You're so true,
Trala trala trala
Tra – lalala – la'

The extraordinary contortions of a couple of mulattoes dancing a kind of nigger cancan added a silent reinforcement to the depressing effect the story had on me.

In this night-tavern, among the painted street-walkers, the brilliantined waiters and the diamond-heeled pimps the whole scene rang hollow and grotesque, collapsing into horrible caricature, only half alive.

As if time, in an unguarded moment, has taken a sudden, silent step, the hours burn away to seconds in our alcoholic daze, blazing like sparks in our soul to illuminate a morbid braid of singular and reckless dreams of past and future, woven out of all sorts of ideas mixed together.

And so I can still hear, from the darkness of recollection, a voice saying: *'We ought to write the Amanita Club a card.'*

I realise now that the conversation must have kept coming back to the same topic.

Other fragments of consciousness gleam in my recollection at intervals: a wineglass smashing, a whistle, a French tart coming to sit on my knee, kissing me, blowing cigarette smoke into my mouth and putting her tongue in my ear. Later someone pushed a very elaborate card under my nose, and I was told to sign it. I dropped the pencil. A second attempt was no good either: the girl tipped a glass of champagne all over my cuff.

I do know quite clearly that we all suddenly sobered up when Lord Hopeless demanded to have the card back, and we turned out our pockets and searched high and low, on the table and under it, to no avail. It had vanished without trace.

> 'Oh, oh Sue,
> You're so true . . .'

screeched the violins as they struck up the chorus, drowning out our awareness of the situation over and over again.

If you closed your eyes you could imagine you were lying on a deep, black velvet rug, dotted with a few ruby-red flowers.

'I want something to eat,' I heard someone say. 'What? — What? — caviare? — don't be stupid. I want — I want — I know, bring me some pickled mushrooms.'

And we all ate some mushrooms and some kind of heavily seasoned cabbage floating in a stringy, watery liquid.

> 'Oh, oh Sue,
> You're so true,
> Trala — trala — trala
> Tra — lalala — la.'

Suddenly, an odd-looking acrobat in a sagging leotard appeared sitting at the table. To his right was a masked hunchback wearing a white flaxen wig. Beside him, a woman; and they were all laughing.

How did he get in, with them? And I turned round: we were the last people left in the room.

Of course, I thought to myself, there wouldn't be anyone else.

It was a very long table we were sitting at, and most of the cloth, clear of plates and glasses, gleamed white.

'Monsieur Phalloides, do give us a dance' said one of the gentlemen, clapping the acrobat on the shoulder.

They know one another, I thought, hauling my imagination back to reality. True, he's probably been sitting there for some time, the – the leotard.

And then I looked at the hunchback next to him, and his eye caught mine. He was wearing a painted white mask and a faded, light green doublet, quite tattered and full of mended patches.

Straight off the street!

His laugh, was a hoarse, wheezing rattle. 'Crotalus – Crotalus horridus': the words came to me out of my schooldays; I could no longer remember what they meant, but I shuddered as I repeated them quietly to myself.

I felt the streetwalker's fingers on my knee under the table.

'My name's Albine Veratrine,' she whispered hesitantly, as if betraying a secret, as I grasped at her hand. She moved closer to me, and I vaguely remembered that she it was who had tipped a glass of champagne over my wrist. Her clothing had such a pungent smell you were almost obliged to sneeze whenever she moved.

'She's called Yeasty of course – Miss Yeasty, you know,' said Dr. Trembler out loud.

The acrobat laughed abruptly, looked at her and shrugged his shoulders as if waiting to make some excuse. I found him repellent: he had a deformity of the skin on his neck like a turkey's wattle, about a hand's-breadth across, all round, and of a pale colour.

His dull flesh-coloured costume hung loose on him, he was so thin and pigeon-chested. He was wearing a flat green cap dotted with white spots and bumps. He had got to his feet and was dancing with someone wearing a necklace of speckled berries.

I see some new ladies have arrived? Lord Hopeless caught my questioning gaze.

'Ignatia, my sister' said Albine Veratrine, and as she said the word 'sister' she winked at me out of the corner of her eye and burst into hysterical laughter.

Then she suddenly put her tongue out at me and I saw with a start of horror a dry, red streak all along its length.

Like some kind of poisonous thing, I thought – why has she got a red streak? A poisonous thing.

And from a distance I heard the music again.

> 'Oh, oh Sue,
> You're so true . . .'

And I could tell, even with my eyes shut, that they were all nodding to the tune.

Poison, I dreamed, and awoke with a cold shudder.

The hunchback in the patchy green doublet had sat a girl on his knee and was peeling off her clothes with angular, jerky movements as if he had St. Vitus' dance. He was listening to the rhythm of some inaudible music.

Dr. Trembler rose heavily to his feet and began to loosen her shoulder-straps.

'Between one second and the next there is always a boundary: it does not exist in time; it is a mere thought, it is like the meshes of a net,' I heard the hunchback say, 'and the totality of these boundaries is still no time at all, and yet we think them, once, again, and again, and a fourth time ... And if we live exclusively within these boundaries, discounting the minutes and the seconds, unaware of them any longer – then we are dead, we are living in death.

You live fifty years: school takes ten: that leaves forty. Twenty are spent asleep: leaves twenty.

Ten are spent worrying – that leaves ten.

For five years it rains: leaving five.

For four of these you worry them away before tomorrow so you live for one year – *perhaps!*

Why do you not wish to die?
Death is beautiful.
It is quiet, always quiet.
And there are no cares for the morrow.
It is the silent present you do not know, no past, no future.
There is the silent present you do not know! The hidden meshes between the seconds in the network of time.'

The hunchback's words sang in my heart and I looked up to see the girl sitting naked on his lap. Her shift had fallen down, but it revealed no body, no breasts – only a phosphorescent fog, from collarbone to hip. And he plunged his fingers into the fog, which rattled like a bass string, and a clatter of limescale pieces poured out.

Death is just so, I felt, just like limescale.

Then the centre of the white tablecloth billowed slowly into the air like a great blister, and an icy draught blew the fog away. Glistening strings came into view, running from the girl's collarbones to her pelvis. This creature was half harp, half woman!

And it seemed to me that the hunchback was harping a refrain of death and the pox upon her, resembling a bizarre hymn:

'So Pleasure turns to pain,
Sure it's not joy again!
You long for pleasure, seek it out;
But all you find and all you pick
Is pain.
And if you've never had that itch
You'll never have the pain to scratch.'

And a great desire for death suddenly overwhelmed me as I listened, and I longed to die.

Yet deep down inside a life stirred, a dark force. Life and death stood opposed in threatening posture: that's what's called paralysis.

My eye never flickered, the acrobat leant across me, and I saw his drooping jersey, his greenish cap and his elaborate ruff.

'Lockjaw,' I tried to stammer through my teeth – in vain.

As he passed from one to another looking slyly into our faces, I knew that we sat in a state of paralysis: he was like a poisonous fungus.

We had eaten poison fungi, along with Veratrum album, the white Hellebore.

All of them spectres of the night!

I tried to cry out loud, but could not.

I tried to turn my head, but could not.

The hunchback in his whitened mask stood up gently, and the others followed him silently, two by two: the acrobat and the French girl, the hunchback and the human harp, Ignatia with Albine Veratrine, and with a tripping cakewalk step they vanished, pair by pair, into the wall. Albine turned just once towards me, and made an obscene gesture.

I tried to turn my eyes or close the lids – I could not. I remained staring at the clock on the wall, watching the hands creeping round the dial like thieving fingers.

And that vulgar couplet rang in my ears again.

> 'Oh, oh, Sue,
> You're so true,
> Trala, trala, trala
> Tra – lalala – la.'

while the Basso ostinato rumbled on beneath:

> 'So pleasure turns to pain,
> And if you've never longed for it
> you'll never feel the pain.'

It was a long while before I got over the poison. The others are all long since buried.

They were beyond saving, I was told, when help came at last.

But I think they were only seeming dead when they were buried, even though the doctor says you don't get tetanus from poison mushrooms; poisoning is different. I suspect they were buried as living dead, and I find myself thinking with a shudder of the Amanita Club, and that spectral hunchback, the *Spotted Arum* with his white mask.

RUPERT'S DROPS

'You see the pedlar over there with the matted beard? They call him Tonio. He'll be coming round to our table in a moment. Buy a little gem from him, or a few Rupert's Drops – you know, those little glass tears that shatter into fragments like salt in your hand when you break off the narrow tail. A mere toy, nothing else. And have a look at his face, and his expression.

Don't you think there's really something very unsettling about the way he looks at you? And in that toneless voice, as he cries his wares. Rupert's Drops, fine-spun ladies' tresses. When we go home I'll tell you the tale of his life – but not here, in this dreary pub: outside, by the lake in the park.

It's a story I'll certainly not forget in a hurry, even if he hadn't once been my friend, though you see him now just as a pedlar, and he no longer recognises me.

Yes, believe me, he was a good friend once, when he was still alive, when he still had his soul and hadn't yet lost his reason. And why don't I help him? It really wouldn't do any good. Don't you think you shouldn't help a poor blind soul find its own way back to the light in its own mysterious way – perhaps to a new and a brighter light?

He's really nothing more than a soul searching for his memory, Tonio here selling Rupert's Drops! You'll see. But let's get away from here.

It's magical, how the lake shines in the moonlight, isn't it! The reeds over there by the bank, so dark and sombre. And look at the way the shadows of the elms rest on the water, over there in that inlet!

Many's the time I have sat on this bank here of a summer's night, listening to the wind whispering in my ear and wheedling its way through the rushes, while the waves splashed sleepily against the tree-roots, and thinking my thoughts down into the secret marvels under the water, where the gleaming fish stir their pink fins as they dream: old, moss-green stones, drowned branches, dead wood and shells shimmering on the white gravel.

Wouldn't it be better to lie dead oneself down there on soft pillows of gently swaying weed, and to forget all this wishing and dreaming?

But I was going to tell you about Tonio.

At that time we were all living up in town: we called him Tonio, though he has another name.

You've probably never heard of Mercedes either. She was beautiful: a Creole, with red hair and such strange, bright eyes.

Where she came from I can't recall now, and she has been gone for a long time.

When Tonio and I met her, at a party at the Orchid Club, she was the mistress of a young Russian fellow.

We were sitting on a veranda, as the distant, limpid tones of some Spanish ballad wafted out to us from the ball-room.

The ceiling had been hung with garlands of tropical orchids of indescribable magnificence. *Cattleya aurea*, the empress of flowers which never dies, Odontoglossas and Dendrobias sprouting from pieces of rotten wood; white, luminous Loelias, like paradise butterflies; cascades of deep blue Lykastas. And out of the thickets of these intertwined blooms there came such an intoxicating scent that I can still sense its pervasive odour when I picture the scene that night, sharp and clear in my mind's eye, as if reflected in a magic mirror: Mercedes reclining on a rough, bark-covered bench, her figure half concealed behind a living curtain of violet Vandeas, her small, expressive face quite hidden in shadow.

None of us spoke a word.

It was like a scene out of the Thousand and One Nights: I was reminded of the tale of the Demon Princess, who would go to the cemetery by moonlight in order to eat the flesh of the dead on the graves. And Mercedes' searching eyes came to rest on me.

A dull recollection welled up inside me, as if once, in far-off times and in a far-distant life, a pair of cold, glittering snake-eyes had fixed me, in a way I would never be able to forget.

She had her head tilted forward, and the fantastic black and purple-speckled tongues of a Burmese Bulbophyllum had become caught in her hair, as if to whisper to her of some novel and outrageous depravity. I realised how possible it would be for a man to give his soul for such a woman.

The Russian lay at her feet. He too was silent.

The party was a strange affair, like the orchids themselves, and full of odd surprises. A negro came in through the double doors carrying a jasper bowl from which he distributed those glittering glass tear-drops invented by Prince Rupert. I saw Mercedes say something to the Russian with a smile, and then he took one of the Drops between his lips, holding it there for a while before offering it to his mistress.

At that very moment a huge orchid sprang away from among the dark mass of foliage behind and reared up, displaying all the features of a demon with greedy, thirsty blubber-lips, no chin, but with glittering eyes and a bluish gaping throat. And this frightful plant-face quivered on its stem, swaying to an evil laugh as it stared at Mercedes' hands. My heart froze, as if my soul had had a glimpse of the abyss.

Do you suppose orchids can think? At that moment I thought they could. I felt, as one with second sight, that these fantastic blooms were gloating as they floated over their mistress's head.

And she was the Orchid-queen, this Creole with the sensuous red lips, shimmering satin-green skin and hair the colour of dead copper. No, indeed no, orchids are not flowers; they are satanic beings, creatures who show us only the tips of their antennae, who merely mimic for us their eyes, lips, tongues in swathes of colour that numb the senses, so that we shan't guess at the existence of the horrific serpent beneath, which, invisible, hides its deadly threat in the realm of shadows.

Intoxicated by the numbing perfume we at last re-entered the ballroom.

The Russian called out his farewells to us – and in truth so they were, for death was waiting behind him. The following morning a boiler-explosion blew him to atoms.

Months went by, and his brother Ivan had become Mercedes' lover, an unapproachable, arrogant fellow, who avoided all contact with the rest of us.

They lived in the villa close by the city gate, and had cut themselves off from all their acquaintances to become submerged in a wild, passionate love-affair.

Whoever saw them, as I did, walking through the park in the evening locked in each other's arms, lost to the world as they conversed in low tones and taking no notice of anything else, would realise that an overpowering passion of a quality quite foreign to us ordinary mortals was holding these two bound to one another.

Then, suddenly, came the news that Ivan, too, had met with an accident. He had apparently taken a balloon flight quite out of the blue and had, inexplicably, fallen from the gondola.

We all thought Mercedes would never survive the blow.

A few weeks later though, in the spring, I saw her ride past me in her open carriage. There was not a trace of the pain she had suffered in her expressionless face. What went past me resembled more an Egyptian Bronze, with its hands resting on its knees and its gaze focussed on another world, than a living woman.

This impression persisted into my dreams: I saw the statue of Memnon with its aura of superhuman stillness and its sightless eyes riding in a modern equipage against the background of a bright dawn, on and on through a glowing purple haze and a swirling mist towards the rising sun; the silhouettes of the wheels and of the horses elongated and oddly distorted, flickering through the dew-damp streets like violet-grey shadows in the pale, early-morning light.

I was away on my own travels for a long time after that, seeing the world and experiencing all sorts of marvellous encounters, yet few of them impressed me so much as this. There do exist particular colours and shapes out of which our souls will readily spin waking and living dreams: the sound of a street grating underfoot at night, the plash of an oar, a stray whiff of perfume, the angular profile of a red roof, raindrops falling on our hands – all these quite often constitute those words of magic that can recall such images to our senses. A deep, melancholy tone reverberates like the echoes of a harp in such sensations of memory.

I returned home and found Tonio as the Russian's successor with Mercedes. Dazed with love, his heart and his senses captivated, he was chained hand and foot, just like his predecessor. I often saw Mercedes and spoke to her: there was the same fathomless love in her too. Sometimes I could feel her gaze resting inquiringly on me.

It was just like that time during the night of the orchid.

Tonio and I would meet occasionally at Manuel's – a mutual friend. And one day I found him sitting there by the window, a shattered soul, his features distorted like one who has been through torture.

Manuel took me silently aside.

It was a remarkable story he told me, in haste, and in a low whisper: Mercedes was a satanist - a witch! Tonio had found this out from letters and other papers he had discovered in her possession. And the two Russians: they had been *murdered* by her, using the magic force of imagination, and with the aid of Rupert's Drops.

I read the manuscript myself, later. The victim, it says there, will be destroyed at the very same moment that the little glass phial, hidden in the mouth and then passed on in a moment of deep emotional intensity during Mass in church, is snapped in two.

And both Ivan and his brother had found just such a sudden and horrific end.

We comprehended Tonio's stark despair.

Even if mere chance were to be held responsible for the success of the sorcery, what an abyss of demonic love lay yet in this woman! A sensibility so exotic and intangible that we mere normal mortals are constrained to sink into a morass of incomprehension if we dare to try to light our way down into these fearful riddles of a cankered soul with any sort of preconception.

We sat then, the three of us, half the night through, listening to the old clock eating the time away, while I searched and searched in vain for any words of comfort: in my brain, in my heart, in my throat. And Tonio's eyes hung unwavering on my lips: he was waiting for the lie that might yet numb his senses.

As Manuel – behind me – took the decision, and opened his mouth to speak, I knew it, without having to turn round. Now, now he would say it. He cleared his throat, his chair scraped on the floor – but then silence came again, ages long. And we felt the lie palpating its way across the room, uncertainly reaching out to touch the walls, like a headless and insubstantial shadow.

Words then at last, mendacious words, dry and withered. 'Perhaps ... perhaps ... she loves you ... differently from the others.'

Absolute silence. We sat and held our breath: if only the lie should not die. It tottered, ready to fall, on jelly-feet: another second, and ...

Slowly, but slowly, Tonio's expression began to change: the phantom of Hope!

The lie had become flesh!

Should I tell you the end? I shudder to put it into words. Come on, let's stand up: there's a cold shiver running down my back. We've stayed here too long sitting on this bench, and the night is so cold.

Look: fate fixes us with its eye like a snake – there is no escape. Tonio descended once more into a mad maelstrom of passion for Mercedes. He walked at her side, he was her shadow. And she with her demonic love held him trapped in her embrace, as an octopus of the sea clasps its victim.

And on Good Friday fate stepped in. Tonio stood, that stormy, early April morning, before the church door, bareheaded, his clothes all torn, and with clenched fists was trying to stop people going in to Mass. Mercedes had written to him, and this had been enough to tip the balance into madness. They found her letter in his pocket: it asked him to give her *one of Prince Rupert's Drops*.

Ever since that Good Friday Tonio's mind has remained imprisoned in ultimate darkness'.

COAGULUM

That eccentric old fellow Hamilcar Baldrian sat lonely at his window and gazed through the panes at the autumnal gloom.

Puffy, dark blue-grey clouds slowly changed shape in the sky, like a shadow-play lazily orchestrated by a giant hand somewhere in the invisible distance.

A blank, sad sunset gleamed through the frosty haze.

Then the clouds sank away to the west, and the glittering stars eyed their way through the mist.

Deep in thought, Baldrian got up and paced the room. What a difficult business this was, calling up spirits. But had he not followed all the instructions to the letter, just as Honorius prescribed in his great *grimoire*? Had he not fasted, watched, anointed himself and recited St. Veronica's little supplication every day?

No, no, it *had* to succeed. Man is supreme on the earth and the powers of Hell are subject to him.

He returned to the window and waited, waited until the cusps of the moon, dull and yellow, thrust up above the frozen branches of the elms.

Then, trembling with anticipation, he lit his old lantern, and started to put together a variety of strange objects he fetched from a cupboard and out of a trunk: magic circles, green wax, a stick surmounted by a crown, dried plants. He tied everything together in a bundle, placed it carefully on the table, and, quietly reciting a prayer, started to undress, until he stood quite naked.

The flickering flame from the lamp cast misleading shadows across the old man's emaciated body with its withered, yellowish skin which tightened, greasily glinting, across his knees, hips and shoulder-blades. His bald skull swayed above his sunken chest, its round and repulsive shadow slipping to and fro across the lime-washed wall, as if in uncertain and anguished pursuit of something.

With a shiver he went across to the stove, and lifted down a glazed earthenware pot, unfastening its rustling shroud as he did so. Its rancid contents released an unpleasant odour. A year ago today he had blended them together: mandrake root, henbane, wax, spermaceti and – he shuddered in disgust – a child's corpse, rendered down into a soup. The woman employed to lay out the dead had sold it to him.

He dipped his fingers hesitantly in the fat and began to smear it over his body, rubbing it into the back of his knees and his armpits. Then he wiped his hands on his chest and pulled on an old, faded and yellowed garment, his 'Heritage Shirt', worn exclusively for magical operations, and replaced the rest of his clothes. The hour was at hand!

A rapid prayer. He reached for the bundle of objects. Just don't forget anything, lest evil gain the power to transform the Treasure at the last moment, when daylight strikes it – Oh, there have been such cases!

Now, wait a moment- copper plate, charcoal dish, tinder for lighting!

Baldrian felt his way unsteadily down the stairs.

In former times the building had been a monastery: now he lived there quite alone, and the local washerwoman brought him whatever he needed every day.

Creaking and groaning, a heavy iron door swung open to reveal a ruinous space. Cellar-stink and thick cobwebs everywhere, rubble piled in the corners, along with the shards of mouldy flowerpots.

A few handfuls of earth carried to the centre of the room – so! (for the feet of the exorcist must stand on soil) – an old chest to sit on, the parchment circle prepared. The name Tetragrammaton on the north side: otherwise the most awful misfortune! Now to light the tinder and charcoal!

What was that?

Rats squeaking, that's all.

Now to cast the plants into the glowing coals – gorse,

nightshade, thorn-apple. Listen how they crackle and smoke!

The old man extinguished his lantern, bent over the bowl and breathed in the venomous smoke; he could scarcely keep his balance, so powerful was its narcotic effect.

And all the time such a frightful roaring in his ears!

With the black wand he prodded at the lumps of wax as they slowly melted on the copper plate, and gathering all his failing forces began in a faltering voice to recite the conjurations of the grimoire:

' . . . true Bread of Heaven and food of the Angels . . . who art the terror of devils . . . though I may be full of foul sinfulness . . . worthy to overcome the ravening wolves and the stinking demons of Hell . . . armour . . . ye hesitate longer in vain . . . Aimaymon Astaroth . . . no longer resist this charm . . . Astaroth . . . I conjure you . . . Eheye . . . Eshereheye.'

He is compelled to sit down, the fear of death is upon him, indefinable, suffocating fear, forcing itself up through the floor, slipping through cracks in the walls, drifting down from above : horrific terror, signalling the approach of the inhabitants of Darkness, consumed with hatred.

The rats are squeaking; but no, no, it is not rats, it is a shrill squeal, fit to split the skull. And then there is the roaring in his ears! It is the sound of the blood in his veins. Or is it not rather the swishing of great wings? The glow of the charcoal fades.

There! Ha! Shadows on the wall. The old man stares, with glazed eyes: just patches of mould, peeling plaster . . .

But then they start to move . . . a death's head, with teeth . . . horns . . . black, empty sockets. Skeletal arms push silently out, a monster begins to emerge from the wall, squatting, filling the whole vault. The skeleton of a vast toad, with the skull of an ox, the bleached bones shining almost visibly from out of the darkness. It is the Demon, Astaroth!

The old man has abandoned his magic circle, and fled

into a corner, cowering against the cold stone of the wall, his tongue paralysed, unable to pronounce the saving command. The hideous, black eye-sockets turn to pursue him, their gaze fixed on his mouth. They it is that have lamed his tongue, he can now only croak in his awful fear.

Slowly, steadily, the spectre creeps forward (he thinks he can hear the scraping of its ribs against the stones) and lifts its toad-claw, groping towards him.

Silver rings, mounted with dull, dusty topaz click against the bony fingers, each linked by a rotting web of skin that wafts at him a terrible odour of decaying flesh.

Now . . . it reaches out to grasp him. Icy shivers seize his heart . . . He tries . . . tries . . . but his senses fail him and he falls forward on his face.

The coals are quenched, a narcotic smoke hangs in the air, billowing slowly across the vault. Through the tiny, barred cellar window the moonlight strikes down, angling into the corner where the old man lies unconscious.

Baldrian is dreaming that he can fly. A violent wind whips at his body. A night-black goat hurtles through the air ahead of him – he can feel its hairy legs right in front of his eyes, its galloping hooves close enough to strike him in the face.

And far, far below him is the earth. Then he feels himself falling, as if through a black satin funnel, down and down, until he finds himself hovering over a landscape spread out below. He knows it well: there is the mossy gravestone, and on the earthy hillock the bare maple with its rigid leafless branches supplicating heaven like fleshless arms. An autumnal frost edges the black swamp-grass.

Shallow pools spread across the waterlogged ground and gleam through the fog like great blind eyes.

Are they not hooded figures, there assembling in the shadow of the gravestone, revealing the glint of weapons, the sparkle of metal buttons and clasps? They gather round for a spectral conference.

A thought flashes across the old man's soul. The Treasure! These are the phantasmal Shades of the Dead, guarding a buried Treasure. And his heart misses a beat in its greed.

He spies down from his hiding place: the earth comes nearer, he is able to grasp the twigs of the tree, gently, gently . . .

There. A withered branch bends and creaks. The dead look up, and see him: he can no longer hold his balance, and he falls, falls into their midst.

His head strikes the gravestone with a thud.

He wakes to the sight of the mildewed patch on the wall, staggers gasping to the door and clambers up the steps, his knees failing under him. He throws himself on the bed, his toothless gums chattering through fear and the cold.

His red felt blanket wraps itself around him, suffocating him, smothering his mouth and hiding his eyes. He tries to turn but cannot, a horrible woollen beast has come to squat on his chest, the winged bat of febrile sleep with huge purple pinions, holding him down, asphyxiating him with its massy weight, forcing him back into the dirty, stuffy pillow.

The old man lay for the whole long winter under the effect of this night, slowly sinking into oblivion. From his sick-bed he gazed across to the little window, where the snow-flakes fled past in an impatient dance, or up at the white ceiling of his room, where a few flies aimlessly paraded.

And when the old tiled stove seemed to give off a smell of scorched juniper berries (oh, what a lung-rending cough he had!) he pictured to himself how in the Spring he would go to uncover the Treasure, out where the old heathen grave was that he had dreamed of, fearing only that the money might yet change and vanish, for the invocation of Astaroth had not quite run to plan.

He had drawn a map of the place on a cover torn from a book: the isolated maple tree, the little moorland pool, and there, X, the Treasure, right next to the worn old grave-stone, that every child was familiar with.

★

The book-cover was now in the hands of the town council, and Hamilcar Baldrian lay outside in the cemetery.

'The old man found a million, but it was too heavy for him to lift out,' went the rumour, and they envied his nephew, a writer and the only heir.

Excavations began: the spot was clearly marked on the plan. A few spadefuls more of earth and – look there – *hurrah, hurrah, a rusty iron chest!*

In triumph it was borne away to the council chamber. Reports were sent to the capital to notify the heir of the discovery and to request the presence of a committee of enquiry, etc.etc.

The tiny railway station swarmed with people – uniformed officials, reporters, detectives, amateur photographers – even the imposing figure of the director of the regional museum appeared, having come down to inspect this interesting plot of land.

They all went off to the heath to gaze for hours into the freshly dug hole, watched over by officers of the Moorland Rangers.

The lush grass of the moor was beaten flat by the mass of patterned rubber soles, but the bright green osiers in their fresh and vivid spring coats winked at one another slyly with their silky catkins, and with each breath of wind quaked in sudden silent laughter, bending their heads to brush the surface of the water. But why?

The toad queen too, plump in her red-spotted coat, sat on her veranda of Ranunculus and Sagittaria drinking in the mild May air. Usually so dignified (she was after all 100003 years old) she was today doubled up with laughter, gaping so wide that her eyes quite disappeared, and waving her left hand wildly in the air. She almost lost a silver topaz ring from her finger.

Meanwhile, the Committee had opened the chest. Such a foul stench greeted their nostrils that for a moment they started back. What strange contents!

An elastic mass, black and yellow, and glutinously shiny.
Suggestions were exchanged, and heads shaken.

'An alchemical preparation, evidently' said the museum director at last. '*Alchemical — alchemical*' — the murmur spread. 'Allchemical? How do you spell that? With three l's? demanded a reporter.

'Ar, it be nobbut a pile o' dung,' says someone else under his breath.

The chest was sealed again, and sent off to the Chemical and Physical Institute with the request for an analysis to be provided, written in ordinary layman's language. All further excavations on the heath bore no fruit; nor did the half-effaced inscription on the gravestone offer further enlightenment: Willi Oberkneifer ††† Lieutenant (Ret.) with below, two carved crossed footprints, probably indicative of some unexplained event in the life of the deceased.

The man had obviously died a hero's death.

The slender means of the inheritor, the author, had been quite depleted by the cost of all this, and the rest was accounted for by the scientific report, which emerged three months later.

This consisted first of several pages devoted to accounts of unsuccessful experiments, followed by a summary of the properties of the mysterious substance, then finally the conclusion: that the mass could in no respect be related to any known material.

So it was worthless! The whole chest not worth a bean! The same evening the poor author was evicted from his room at the inn. The affair of the Treasure seemed to be at an end.

But one more excitement was in store for the town. The following morning the poet might have been seen running hatless and with flowing mane through the streets to the Council Offices. 'I know it, I know it,' he was shouting, over and over again. A crowd grew round him. 'What do you know?'

'I spent the night on the heath,' he gasped, breathless, 'and a spectre appeared to me, and told me what it was. In the old days ... there were so many Honour Courts ... held out there, and ...'

'Devil take it, what about the stuff?' roared one of the bystanders. The poet continued:

'Specific gravity 23, shiny surface, bicoloured, fragmented into the tiniest particles and yet as sticky as pitch, unusually flexible, penetrating ...'

The crowd was losing patience: all that had been described in the scientific analysis.

'Well, the spirit said to me it was a *fossilized, solidified officer's word of honour!* And I have just written to the bank to convert this curiosity into cash.'

Then they fell silent, laid hands on him, and saw that he was talking nonsense.

But who knows if the poor fellow might not gradually have regained his sanity when the answer to his letter arrived:

'Regretfully we have to inform you that we are unable to make any advance, nor offer you any cash equivalent for the article in question, since we are unable to describe it as an object of any value, even were it not fossilized or coagulated. We suggest that you make enquiry of a Waste Products Valuation Agency.

Respectfully,

A.B.C. Wucherstein & Co. Bankers'

So he slit his throat.

And now he rests alongside his uncle, Hamilcar Baldrian.

THE SECRET OF HATHAWAY CASTLE

Ezekiel von Marx was the best somnambulist I have ever met.

Quite often he would fall into a trance right in the middle of a conversation, and would then speak of events that were occurring in far away places or which would occur only days or weeks later, and all with an exactness that would have done honour to a Swedenborg.

How would it be possible, then, to induce such a trance in Marx, deliberately, and just when you wanted it?

Last time we had met, my six friends and I, we had tried every possible means: we had spent the whole evening trying experiments with hypnotic passes, laurel smoke etc., but nothing had succeeded in putting Ezekiel von Marx to sleep.

'Waste of time,' said Mr. Dowd Gallagher (a Scot) at last. 'You can see it's no good. I'll tell you something instead, something so remarkable you'd spend day and night trying to work the riddle out, to explain the inexplicable.

It's almost a year now since I heard about it, and not a day has passed but I've wasted hours trying to construct an explanation that is halfway plausible. As a writer I staked my pride on finding a hypothesis at least, but it's been all to no purpose, even though I know every key to both Western and Eastern occultism, you know I do! So, let's see if *you* can find the solution to this story, if you can: it would impress me! Just listen to this,' and he cleared his throat:

'From time immemorial, as far back as the family history of the Earls of Hathaway extends, the same dark fate overcomes the firstborn in every succeeding generation. A deathly frost casts a pall on the life of the eldest son on the very day he reaches his 21st year, and it never leaves him again until his dying day.

Withdrawn, taciturn, brooding in sorrow, out hunting alone all day, they pass their lives away at Hathaway Castle until their own eldest child, having now come of age, relieves them in accordance with the law and accepts the mantle of his lamentable inheritance. Formerly so full of joy the young Earls are changed at a stroke and, if they have not already managed to become engaged to be married, the task of bringing a wife home to their cheerless hearth becomes a near impossibility.

Yet not one of them has ever attempted suicide: all this misery and depression, which has never deserted them, not for a single moment, has nevertheless been insufficient to sow the seed of self-destruction in even just one of them.

I had a dream once, in which I found myself lying on an Island of the Dead – one of those Mohammedan burial places in the Red Sea, where the withered trees shine white in the sun as if drenched in milk-white froth – a froth consisting of millions of vultures, patiently waiting.

I was lying on the sand, unable to move. An indescribable and frightful smell of warm decay wafted over me, drifting out from the island's interior. Night fell, and the ground came alive. Translucent crabs of an awesome size came scurrying across the sand out of the sea, grown hypertrophic on a diet of human corpses.

And I dreamed that one came and sat on my neck, sucking out all the blood.

I couldn't see it – it was outside the range of my vision: there was just a dull bluish cast on my chest falling from my shoulder, where the moonlight shone through the transparent monster, which was so insubstantial that it scarcely threw a shadow at all.

So I prayed in my soul to the Master, that he should in his mercy extinguish my life's flame.

I started to calculate when my blood supply would run out, and clutched at the hope that the sun was bound to bring, along with the far distant morning. I think that the light of a faint hope must similarly glimmer for the Earls of Hathaway, just as in my dream, in the midst of their endless and miserable gloom.

You see, I became personally acquainted with the present Lord Vivian when he was still Viscount Arundale. He spoke a great deal about this fate that was overhanging him, since his 22nd birthday was not far off, and added boldly with a laugh that the plague itself, if it were to confront him directly with its livid face and make a play for his very life, would not succeed in securing even one hour of his carefree youth.

We were in Hathaway Castle at the time. The old Earl had gone hunting in the mountains, and had been away for weeks – I never met him. His wife, Lady Ethelwyn, Vivian's mother, doleful and distraught, hardly spoke to us at all.

One exception occurred when I was sitting alone with her on the veranda, and to cheer her up I was telling her about all the madcap antics and wild jokes of her Vivian, to show how they were the best proof of his almost indestructible cheerfulness and carefree spirit. She began to thaw a little, and started to tell me all sorts of things about the curse which she had read of in the family records or had seen and discovered for herself in the course of her long and lonely marriage.

I spent the night after this quite unable either to sleep or to banish the strange and frightful images which her words had conjured up in my mind's eye.

In the castle there was, she said, a secret room, the hidden entrance to which was known only to the Earl and his Steward, a sinister and gloomy old man. The young heir was bound, at the vital moment, to step across its threshold. He would stay there for twelve hours and he would then emerge, a pale and broken figure.

Lady Ethelwyn had once had the idea of ordering a piece of linen to be hung at every window, and by this means she had found that one window remained undecorated, and this of course belonged to the room with the undiscoverable door. Further investigation was however fruitless. The labyrinthine old corridors of the castle defeated every attempt to find the way to it.

At times, however, and always at the same season of the year, everyone was struck by an uncertain but oppressive sense that an invisible guest had arrived for a sojourn in the Castle. It was a sense that gradually - perhaps reinforced by a certain series of imponderable signs – grew to be a dreadful certainty.

And one night, lit by the full moon, when Lady Ethelwyn, plagued by sleeplessness and fear, had looked out into the courtyard, she saw with a feeling of ineffable terror the steward, stealthily leading along a ghostly, ape-like figure of appalling ugliness, which all the while emitted rattling, croaking sounds.'

Mr. Dowd Gallagher fell silent, passed a hand across his brow, and leaned back.

'I am still haunted by the scene today' he continued, 'and I can picture the old castle, built in the shape of a square block and set in a clearing of the park, and flanked by gloomy oaks planted in oddly curving lines.

And as if in a vision I can see the gothic windows, each with its scrap of washing on display, and with a dark, empty space in the middle. And then – then . . .

Oh yes, something else I forgot to mention: whenever the presence of the invisible visitor becomes palpable, a faint and inexplicable aroma permeates the corridor – one old retainer described it as smelling something like onions. What could it all mean?

A few weeks after I had left Hathaway Castle, news reached me that Vivian had grown morose. So now it was his turn! This daredevil, who would have squared up to a tiger with his bare fists! Tell me, have you got any explanation, gentlemen?

If it had been a ghost, a curse, a magic spectrum, the plague in person, for Heaven's sake, Vivian would at least have made some attempt to resist . . .'

The crash of a broken glass interrupted the narrator. We

looked up, startled: Ezekiel von Marx was sitting bolt upright, stiff in his seat, his eyes focussed on infinity, a somnambulist. His wine glass had fallen from his hand.

At once I placed myself in magnetic contact with him, stroking his solar plexus and addressing him in a whisper.

Soon his state of mind was such that we could all communicate with him in the form of short questions and answers, and the following conversation ensued:

Myself: Have you something to say to us?

Ezekiel v. Marx: Feiglstock.

Mr. D. Gallagher: What's that?

E v M: Feiglstock.

Another gent: Please make yourself clearer.

E v M: Feiglstock, Attila. Banker. Budapest. 7 The Boulevard.

Mr. D.G.: I don't understand a word.

Myself: Has this got anything to do with Hathaway Castle?

E v M: Yes.

Gent in Dinner Jacket: What is the ape-like figure in the courtyard with the croaking voice?

E v M: Dr. Max Lederer.

Myself: Not Feiglstock, then?

E v M: No.

The Painter Kubin: Who is Dr. Max Lederer then?

E v M: Lawyer and associate of Feiglstock, Attila, Banker in Budapest.

A third gent: What is Dr. Lederer doing in Hathaway Castle?

E v M: (Mumbles something incomprehensible.)

Kubin: What have the Earls of Hathaway to do with Feiglstock's bank?

E v M: (Whispering, in deep trance) From the start. Business friends of the Earls.

Myself: What initiation were the heirs to the title put through on that particular day?

E v M: (Silent)

Myself: Answer the question, if you please.

E v M: (Silent)

Gent in dinner Jacket [*Loudly*]: What were they initiated into?

E v M [*Laboriously*]: Into the fam-i-ly bank ac-count.

Mr. D.G [*thoughtfully*]: Of course! *Into the fam-i-ly bank account!*

CHIMERA

The grey stones stand bathed in the warm sunlight – the old square is dreaming away a quiet Sunday afternoon.

The tired houses with their worn and decaying wooden steps lean slumbrously against one another, hiding secluded corners. Inside, old-fashioned parlours stand solidly furnished with good mahogany pieces.

And the warm summer air wafts in through watchful open windows.

A solitary figure can be descried, walking across the square towards St. Thomas' Church, whose tower gazes devoutly down on this tranquil scene.

He passes inside, and encounters an aroma of incense.

The heavy door sighs back onto its leather stop, and the loud glare of the world is swallowed up. The rays of the sun filter down greenish pink through the narrow lancets on to the sacred paving. Underneath the pious lie at rest from the ceaseless bustle of existence.

He breathes in the dead air. Every sound has faded away. The church lies rapt in the shadow of sound.

His pulse slows as his heart absorbs the dark, incense-laden air.

The stranger looks at the ranks of pews, each inclined devotionally towards the Altar, as if waiting upon a coming miracle.

Here is one of those beings who has overcome his pain, and who sees with different eyes deep into another world. He feels the mysterious breath of things, the secret, silent life of the half-light.

Unacknowledged, hidden thoughts born here drift uneasily, questing through this enclosed space. Existences without blood, without joy or sorrow, pale as wax, like the sickly outgrowths of darkness.

The red lamps swing silently, solemnly, at the end of

long, patient cords. They move in the draught from the wings of the golden archangel.

There! A gentle scraping sound under the benches, and something scurries across into concealment under the prie-dieu.

But now, here it comes sidling round the columns.

A livid human hand!

It scuttles across the floor on its agile fingers, a ghostly spider.

Listen. Now it's climbing up an iron post, and vanishing into the offertory box.

The silver coins inside clink gently against one another.

The solitary man, in abstracted mood, has been following it with his eyes, until his gaze now falls on an old man standing in the shadow of a pillar. Each looks earnestly at the other.

'There are many greedy hands here,' whispers the old man.

The other nods his agreement.

Dim figures slowly materialise out of the nocturnal gloom, barely moving.

Prayersnails!

Human busts: mysterious outlines of women's veiled heads superimposed on cold, slimy snail bodies, with black, catholic eyes, sucking noiselessly across the chill pavement.

'They live on empty prayers,' says the old man. 'Everyone sees them, yet nobody knows them as they crouch by day at the church doors.'

When the priest reads Mass they sleep in whispering corners.

'Am I disturbing your prayers?' asks the solitary.

The old man comes to join him, and stands to his left: 'He whose feet stand in living water, he is himself prayer! But I knew that someone would come today who can *see* and *hear*!'

Yellow reflections of light flit across the stones, like will o' the wisps.

192

'Can you see the veins of gold running under the paving?'

The old man's face flickers.

The other shakes his head: 'My gaze does not delve so deep. Or do you mean something else?'

The old man takes his hand and leads him to the altar.

The image of Christ on the Cross towers silently above. Shadows shift quietly in the dark side-chapels, behind swelling ornamental railings; shades of old convent sisters from forgotten times past, never to return, outlandish figures, submissive as the scent of incense.

Their black silk habits rustle as they move.

The old man points to the floor. 'It nearly reaches the surface here. Just a foot down beneath the stones; pure gold, a broad, gleaming band. The veins run across the old square far under the houses. Extraordinary, that people didn't stumble across it long ago, when they laid the pavement. I alone have known it for many years, and have never told anyone, until today. None of them had a pure heart.

A sound!

Inside the glass reliquary the silver heart held in the bony hand of St. Thomas has suddenly fallen. The old man has not heard it. He is far away: his eyes look ecstatically into the distance with a firm and steady gaze.

'Those who come now shall beg no more. A temple will rise, of shimmering gold. The ferryman is coming across — for the last time.'

The stranger hearkens to the prophetic words, whose whispered tones penetrate into his soul like the fine, suffocating dust accumulating from the sanctified decay of vanished centuries.

Here beneath his feet! A shining sceptre of chained and slumbering power! His eyes begin to burn: *must* the curse lie on the gold? Can it not be lifted through human love and compassion? How many thousands are starving!

From the tower above the bell strikes seven. The air quivers.

The solitary man's thoughts fly with the sound of the bell out into a world filled with extravagant art, full of pomp and magnificence.

He shudders, and looks at the old man. How the space has changed! His footfall echoes. The corners of the pews have been broken off, the bases of the pillars worn away. The white-painted statues of the popes are covered in dust.

'Have you ... have you seen the metal with your own eyes ... have you held it in your hand?'

The old man nods agreement. 'In the cloister-garden outside, near the statue of Mary Mother of God, amongst the flowering lilies, there you can reach it.'

He pulls out a blue box: 'Here.' He opens it and gives the other something covered in lumpy projections.

The two men are silent.

The hubbub of life from far away penetrates into the church. The people are returning from a happy day out in the country meadows – tomorrow they must return to work.

The women carry their weary children on their arms.

The solitary man has accepted the thing, and now he shakes the old man by the hand. Then he casts a look back at the altar. Once more a mysterious breath of tranquil recognition envelops him.

'Things start from the heart : born in the heart, fitted to the heart.'

He puts a hand to the Cross, and goes. The exhausted day leans the door ajar, and a fresh evening breeze wafts in.

A cart rattles across the market square, bedecked with foliage and filled with a laughing, happy crowd, while through the arches of the old houses the red rays of the setting sun beam down.

The stranger stops to lean on the stone monument in the middle of the square and drifts into a reverie. In spirit he calls across to the passers-by to tell them what he has just learned, and he hears the laughter die away. The buildings fall to dust, the church collapses. Uprooted, lying in the dust, the tearful lilies of the cloister-garden.

The earth shakes: the demons of hate are bellowing to Heaven!

A pounding hammer beats and pulverises the square, the town, and all the bleeding human hearts into golden dust.

The dreamer shakes his head and ponders, listening to the melodious voice of the hidden Master in his heart:-

'He who is not afraid of a wicked deed and who does not care for one that offers happiness –

He it is who is resigned, discerning and resolute, full of essentiality.'

But this lumpy thing in his hand is surely too light for solid gold?

– The solitary man glances down at what he holds:

It is a human vertebra!

A SUGGESTION

23rd September

So, I've finished my system and I'm certain that I shall not feel afraid.

The secret code is indecipherable. It's good when you have managed to think out everything in advance, and are at the pinnacle of knowledge in as many ways as possible. This will be my diary; no-one else can read it, and I can set down whatever seems necessary in my process of self-observation. Concealment on its own won't do: chance will bring things to light.

It's precisely the most elaborate concealment that is the least safe. What you learn in childhood is all so upside down! But over the years I have come to learn how to see into the heart of things, and I know exactly what I have to do to avoid any trace of fear.

Some say conscience exists, others deny it; that means it is a problem for both and a cause of conflict. And yet, how simple the truth is: conscience exists, or it doesn't, according to whether you believe in it or not. If I believe I have a conscience, it is because I have suggested the idea to myself. Obviously.

It's only odd that, if I do believe in conscience, it not only comes into existence *because* of that, it also manages to set itself up quite independently *against* my own desire and my own will.

Set 'against'! That's odd. The 'I' that I imagine sets itself against the 'I' with which I have created it, and acts out then a completely independent role.

And this seems to be the case with other things actually, too. For example, my heart sometimes beats faster when people talk of murder, with me standing there, and yet I'm sure they can't find me out. I'm not remotely frightened in such cases, – I know exactly, for I watch myself too closely for it not to escape my notice; and yet I can feel my heart beating faster.

This idea about conscience is quite the most devilish a priest can ever have thought of.

I wonder who it was who first dreamed it up? A sinner? Hardly. An innocent? A so-called righteous man? How would such a one be able to think through the consequences of the idea? It can only be that some old man or other imagined it as a nightmare to frighten the children; with an instinctive sense of the impending defencelessness of age in the face of the burgeoning power of brutal youth.

I can remember well how as a youth I still thought it was possible that the shade of the victim could fasten itself to a murderer's heels and appear to him in visions.

Murderer! Just think how clever they were to choose that word. Think of the sound. There's really something of a death-rattle in it.

It's the repeated 'ur' – sound that expresses the horror. How cleverly people have wrapped us round in suggestions!

But I know how to counter such dangers. I repeated the word to myself that evening a thousand times over, until it lost its horror for me. Now it's just a word like any other.

I can well imagine that some unprepared murderer might be hounded into madness by imagining he's being pursued by his victim; but it would only be someone who doesn't think, doesn't consider, and isn't forearmed.

Who nowadays is accustomed to gazing cold-bloodedly straight into a dying eye and to catching its overwhelming fear of death; without being aware of a crack in the shell, or throttling the curse stuck in a choking throat, a curse of which one is secretly afraid? No wonder that such an image may *come alive*, and create a kind of conscience which will eventually destroy you.

When I consider myself I have to concede that I set about the business like a genius:

To poison two people one after the other, and to remove

every trace of suspicion – people less smart than I have been have managed to do that. But to smother guilt, one's own feelings of guilt, even before they are born, now that . . .

I really think I am the only one . . .

Yes, if ever anyone had the bad luck to be omniscient, he would have trouble building an inner defence. But I took advantage of my own ignorance, and chose a poison whose effect creates a kind of death that is and shall remain quite unknown to me.

Morphine, Strychnine, Potassium cyanide – I either know, or can imagine, their effects: spasms, cramps, sudden collapse, foaming at the mouth.

But Curare! I have no idea what death-throes this poison induces, and how should I find out? I shall, of course, avoid reading about it; and to hear something about it, either by chance or involuntarily, is out of the question. Who nowadays even knows the name?

So, if I can't even picture the last minutes of my two victims (what a stupid word) how could such an image pursue me? And if I should dream about it, I can directly *prove* to my own satisfaction when I wake, that such a suggestion is untenable. And what suggestion could be stronger than such a *proof*?

26th September

Remarkable. Last night I distinctly dreamed of my two dead victims walking to left and right behind me. Perhaps it's because I wrote down that idea about dreaming yesterday.

There are just two ways now of blocking off such visions: either you keep them before your mind's eye, to get used to them, as I did with the word 'murderer', or else you wipe the recollection out of your memory completely.

The first? Well, the vision was too awful. I'll choose the second. So: I will not think about it any more. I will not. I will *not not not* think any more about it. Do you hear! You won't think any more about it!

In fact the phrase 'you will not' etc. is altogether ill-advised, as I now realise: you shouldn't use the form 'you' to address yourself – you divide yourself into two parts by doing so – an 'I' and a 'you' - and in time that could have disastrous consequences!

5th October

If I hadn't studied the nature of suggestion so exactly I could become really nervous. Last night was the eighth time I have had the same dream. Always the two of them behind me, right on my heels. I shall go out tonight, join the crowds and drink rather more than usual. I'd like to go to the theatre most of all - but of course, tonight it's *Macbeth*.

7th October

You're always learning something new. Now I know why I was bound to dream of it so persistently. Paracelsus says quite expressly that if one regularly wants vivid dreams, one need do nothing else but write one's dreams down once or twice. I'll make sure I leave that out. I wonder if a modern expert would know that. But they all know straight away how to take issue with Paracelsus, don't they?

13th October

I must write down exactly what happened today, so that nothing can take root in my recollection that never actually happened.

For some time I have had the feeling (I've got rid of the dreams, thank goodness) that someone has been following behind me, on the left.

I could, of course, have turned round, to convince myself I was imagining it, but that would have been a great mistake, because by doing so I would have implicitly admitted the *possibility* of there really being something there.

This has been going on for some days and I have been on my guard. When I came down to breakfast this morning I had this tiresome feeling again, and then suddenly I heard a crunching noise behind me. Before I could pull myself together I had swung round in fright, and for a split second I saw absolutely clearly the dead shape of Richard Erben, grey against grey, before the phantom slipped behind me again in a flash. But it's not so far away that I can't feel it there, as before. If I stand quite straight and turn my eyes to the left as far as they will go, I can see its contour just on the edge of my vision. If I turn my head, the figure moves back to the same extent.

It's obvious that the noise can only have been made by my old cleaning woman, who is always bustling about the doorways, never still for a moment.

From now on I shall only let her come in when I am not at home. I categorically want nobody near me any more.

How my hair stood on end! I think that must be caused by a contraction of the skin on the head.

And the phantom? My first thought was that it was an echo of the earlier dreams, quite simply, and that its visible manifestation occurred as a result of the sudden fright. Fright – fear, hatred, love are simply forces that divide the ego, and are consequently able to make one's own thoughts visible when they are otherwise quite unconscious, so that they reflect themselves in one's perceptive capacity as if in a mirror.

I haven't been able to mingle with other people for a long time now. I have to watch myself carefully. I mustn't let it get any worse.

It's unfortunate that all this had to happen just on the thirteenth of the month. I really ought to have made a point of putting up a strong defence against that stupid prejudice against the thirteenth right from the start, since I seem to be affected by it too. Though there's nothing in that quite unimportant circumstance anyway.

20th October

I wish I could pack up my bags and go somewhere else. The old woman has been fussing round the door again. I've heard the noise again. Behind me and to the right this time. The same affair as before. This time on the right-hand side I can see the uncle I poisoned. And If I push my chin down on my chest and squint at my shoulders I can see one on each side. I can't see their legs. As a matter of fact, I have the impression that the figure of Richard Erben is clearer, as if he is closer to me. The old woman will have to go. Things are getting more and more suspicious, but I shall go on for a few more weeks being nice to her, so as to allay her doubts.

I shall have to put off moving for a while too. People would notice, and you can't be too careful.

Tomorrow I'll repeat the word 'murderer' for a few hours. It's started to make me feel uncomfortable, so I must get used to the sound again.

I made a remarkable discovery today; I looked at myself in the mirror and noticed that I'm walking on the ball of my foot more than I used to, which makes me sway a little. The phrase 'to put a firm foot forward' seems to have a deep, inner meaning – indeed there seems to be some psychological secret contained in words altogether. I must be careful to use my heels more.

God, if only I didn't forget overnight a full half of what I intend to do during the day! Purely as if sleep just wiped it away.

1st November

I deliberately said nothing last time about the other phantom, but it still won't go away.

It's horrible, horrible. Is there nothing I can do to fend them off?

Once I quite clearly worked out two ways of escaping visions of that sort. I chose the second and yet I always find myself on the first. Was I mentally deranged then? Are these two figures splinters from my ego, or have they got an independent existence?

No, No! If that were the case I would be feeding them with my own life! So they really exist! Dreadful! But no, it's just that I *see* them as independent entities, and what one sees as reality is ... is ... Oh, merciful God, I'm not even writing normally! I'm writing as if someone were dictating it to me. That must be the result of writing in code, which I always have to translate first before I can read it properly.

Tomorrow I shall write out the whole book again in my normal script.

Oh God, stay with me in this long night.

10th November

They are *real* beings. They told me about their death-throes in my dreams. Jesus protect me, ah, Jesus, Jesus! They're going to strangle me! I looked it up, and it's true, Curare works like that, just like that. How would they know that, if they were merely apparitions?

God in Heaven, why did you never tell me that people live on after death? I wouldn't have committed the murders.

Why didn't you reveal yourself to me when I was a child? I'm writing again just in the way people talk; and I don't want to.

12th November

Now that I've written out the whole book again I can see clearly that I'm ill. A steady spirit and a clear head is what's wanted.

I've asked Dr. Wetterstrand to see me in the morning, to tell me exactly where I went wrong. I'll tell him everything in the minutest detail, he will listen to me quietly and tell me what I don't yet know about suggestion.

For one thing he can't possibly believe that I really have killed someone. He'll just think I'm mad.

And I'll make sure he doesn't get the chance to think about it anymore when he gets home.

A little glass of wine will do the trick!

13th November

----------------------------------- 0.50t

THE INVALID

The day-room in the sanatorium was crowded, as usual; everyone sitting there motionless, waiting for their health to arrive.

There was no conversation: they were all afraid of hearing some account of their neighbour's illness, or doubts being expressed about their own treatment.

It was unspeakably desolate and boring, and the dull slogans in shiny black German lettering pasted onto white cards on the walls made you want to vomit.

A little boy was sitting at the table opposite me. I was obliged to keep staring at him, because otherwise I would have had to move my head to an even more uncomfortable position.

Dressed in a tasteless style, and with his low forehead, he looked altogether stupid. His mother had sewn bits of white lace to his velveteen cuffs and trouser-legs.

Time lay heavily on us all – like an octopus sucking us dry. I wouldn't have been surprised if suddenly all these people had leaped up in unison, without any particular immediate cause, and with a cry of rage had torn everything to pieces – tables, windows, lamps.

I couldn't really understand why I didn't do it; perhaps it was because I was afraid the others wouldn't join in, and I would have to sit down again shamefacedly.

Then I caught sight of the lace trimmings again, and felt the boredom becoming even more excruciating and oppressive. I had the feeling I was holding a huge grey rubber ball in my mouth, and it was getting bigger all the time and growing into my brain.

At such moments of desolation, oddly enough, even the thought of any change is an abomination.

The boy was arranging dominoes in a box and then feverishly taking them out again, only to put them back once more in a different order. There were no more left over, and yet the box wasn't quite full, as he had hoped. There was still room for one whole extra row.

He started tugging roughly at his mother's arm at last, pointing in frustration at this asymmetry, and saying, simply: 'Mama, mama!' His mother had just been talking to her neighbour about the servant problem and similar serious matters such as concern the feminine mind, and was now gazing blankly, like a rocking-horse, at the box.

'Put the tiles in the other way round,' she said.

A gleam of hope passed across the child's face, and he set about this task once more with laborious delight.

Another age passed.

Nearby a newspaper page crackled.

The sententious exhortations on the cards caught my eye again. I felt I was going to go mad.

Now! now – the feeling came to me from outside, it jumped at my head, like an executioner.

I stared at the boy. It was coming over to me from him. The box was now full, and yet there was one tile left over! The boy almost dragged his mother off her chair. She had been going on about servants again, and now she stood up, saying: 'It's bed-time now, you've been playing long enough.'

The boy said nothing, but stared about, wild-eyed, the most vivid illustration of a state of desperation I have ever seen.

I turned in my armchair and wrung my hands. I too had caught the infection.

They both left, and I could see that it was raining outside. How much longer I sat there, I do not know.

I dreamed of all the most miserable experiences of my life. They looked at each other with black domino-eyes, as if searching for something or other, and I was trying to lay them out in a green coffin. But every time I tried to do so there were either too many of them – or too few.

G.M.

'That old bastard Mackintosh is back'

The news ran through the city like wildfire.

The memory of George Mackintosh, German-American, who had bade farewell to everyone five years ago, was still fresh in everyone's mind. His trickery was no more forgettable than his dark hatchet-face, that had turned up on the Parade.

'What's he up to, back here again?'

He had been slowly but surely edged out: everybody had played a part in that – the one with an expression of friendship, another using malice and false rumours, all of them using a certain element of circumspect slander. All these little humiliations eventually added up to such treatment as would probably have crushed the spirit of any other man, but which in this case merely persuaded the American to take a trip abroad.

Mackintosh had a face as sharp as a paper-knife, and very long legs. That in itself is hard for people to stomach who have no regard for racial theory.

He was truly the object of hatred, but instead of reducing it by taking steps to conform to conventional ideas, he would always stand aside from the crowd, and was always coming up with something new: hypnosis, spiritism, palmistry – indeed, one day he even produced a symbolist reading of *Hamlet*. That got the good citizens of the town excited of course, especially budding geniuses like Herr Tewinger of the *Daily*, who was just about to publish a book with the title: *What I think about Shakespeare*.

And this veritable 'thorn in the flesh' had come back, and was living at the 'Sun' with his Indian servant.

'Just passing by?' asked an old acquaintance tentatively. 'Of course, but only very temporarily. I can't move in to my house until August 15th. I've bought a house in Ferdinand Street, you know.'

The whole face of the town fell by an inch. A house in Ferdinand Street! Where did this mountebank get the money? And an Indian servant, too. Well, we'll see how long *he* lasts!

Mackintosh had yet another scheme, of course. An electrical device that could as it were sniff out veins of gold in the ground. A kind of modern divining rod.

Naturally, most people didn't believe it. 'If it were any good someone else would have thought of it already!'

It was not to be denied, though, that the American must have become incredibly rich in the last five years.

That at least was the firm and unshakeable opinion of the information office of Messrs. Snooper & Son-in-law.

It was true. Not a week went by but he bought another house.

All over the place, too: one in the Fruit Market, another in Lordship Lane – but all in the inner city.

For heaven's sake, was he trying to become Mayor or something? Nobody could hazard a guess as to what he was up to.

'Have you seen his visiting cards at all? Look here, it's the very limit! Just a monogram, no name. He says he doesn't need to be called by a name anymore, he has money enough!'

Mackintosh had gone off to Vienna, and (so it was reported) was spending his days in conclave with a series of parliamentary deputies queuing up to see him.

What deep plans he was hatching with them was altogether unascertainable, but he evidently had a hand in the new draft law concerning amendments to prospecting rights.

There was something about this in the papers every day, presenting arguments for and against, and it was beginning to look as though the law, which would permit free prospecting rights even in urban areas (apart, that is, from the usual excavations of course), would soon be brought into effect.

The whole business looked most peculiar: the general opinion was that some big coal firms must be behind it.

Mackintosh on his own surely had no such great interest in the matter – he was probably only a front for some conglomerate or other.

Whatever the case, he soon came back home and seemed to be in the best of spirits. Nobody had ever seen him behaving so affably.

'He's really doing well – he bought another piece of real estate only yesterday – the thirteenth' said the Chief Executive of the Land Registry at the table reserved for public officials in the Casino. 'You know the one, on the corner, the 'Despairing Virgin', diagonally across from the 'Three Absolute Idiots', where the Central Inventory Commission for the Regional Inundations Inspectorate has its city offices.

'The man will overreach himself yet,' observed the surveyor. 'Do you know what he's asking for now, gentlemen? – He wants to demolish three of his houses – the one in Pearl Alley, the fourth on the right by the Gunpowder Tower, and Requisition No. 47184/II. The new designs have already been approved.'

Mouths fell open.

The autumn wind swept through the streets : nature was drawing a deep breath before settling down to sleep.

The sky is so blue and cold, the clouds so full and cheeky, the scene so idyllic, as if the dear Lord had had the whole thing painted by Wilhelm Schulz . . . How pure and beautiful the town would be if only that frightful American in his mania for destruction hadn't polluted the clear air so much with brick-dust. But to think that such a thing has even been approved!

To pull down three houses – well and good, but all thirteen together: that's beyond a joke!

Everyone's coughing, and it hurts like the devil when you get that damned dust in your eyes.

'It'll be some kind of monstrosity he puts in their place. 'Neo-modern' of course, I bet,' they said.

'You can't have heard right, surely, Herr Schebor! What? He's not going to build anything? Is he mad – why on earth did he put in the new building plans?' 'Simply to get provisional permission to demolish!'

'Now you know the latest, gentlemen', panted Vyskotschil, aspiring castle-builder, quite out of breath. 'There's gold in the city, yes, gold. Possibly right under our feet.'

Everyone looked down at Vyskotschil's feet, flat as pancakes in his patent-leather boots.

The whole neighbourhood of the Parade came running.

'Who said something about gold?' cried the broker Löwenstein.

'Mr. Mackintosh says he has found gold ore in the ground under the house he pulled down in Pearl Alley,' confirmed a man from the Ministry of Mines. 'They've even wired for a Commission to come down from Vienna.'

A few days later George Mackintosh was the most celebrated man in town. There were photographs of him in all the shops – with his angular profile, his mocking expression and his narrow lips.

The papers were full of biographical details, the sports correspondents suddenly knew all about his weight, his chest size and his biceps, even his lung capacity.

It wasn't difficult to get an interview with him, either.

He was back at the 'Sun', gave everyone admittance, offered them the most marvellous cigarettes and told, with delightful generosity, what had led him to destroy his houses and to dig for gold in the cleared site.

With his new apparatus, his own invention, which could indicate the presence of gold in the earth by the variation in an electric current, he had by night thoroughly investigated not only the cellars of his *own* buildings, but those (having secretly gained access to them) of all his neighbours as well.

'Look, here are the official reports of the Mining Ministry, and an opinion from the eminent Professor Upright of Vienna – who incidentally is an old friend of mine.'

And indeed there, in black and white, and authenticated by the official stamp, was confirmation that on all thirteen sites purchased by the American George Mackintosh gold existed in the familiar form in admixture with sand, in proportions which suggested that an immense quantity was certainly present, especially at deeper levels. This kind of distribution had so far been proved to exist only in America and Asia, but Mr. Mackintosh's opinion that what we had here was an old, prehistoric river bed could be agreed without further ado. A precise valuation was, of course, impossible to put into figures, but that this was a hidden deposit of metal of outstanding proportions – perhaps even unexampled, could not be doubted.

The American's plan of the probable extent of the gold-mine was particularly interesting, and had won total acceptance from the Expert Committee.

It now became evident that the former river-bed ran from one of the American's houses to the rest through a complicated series of bends via other properties until it disappeared beneath Mackintosh's corner house in Zettner Lane.

The proof that this was the case and that it could not be otherwise was so simple and clear that it was obvious to everyone, even those unwilling to believe in the ability of the electric machine to identify metals accurately.

What luck, that the new prospecting right had already passed into law. How prudently and discreetly the American had provided for everything. The owners of the land under which such wealth was suddenly to be found presided pompously in the cafes, full of praise for their inventive neighbour, whom they had earlier traduced so vilely and unjustifiably.

'Shame upon such slanderers!'

Every evening they attended long meetings, and sat in conclave with the legal advisor to the Select Committee, discussing what to do next.

'Quite simple! – Do everything Mr. Mackintosh does,' was his advice. 'Submit new building plans, as many as you like, as required by law, then demolish, demolish, demolish, so that you can get at the land as quickly as possible. There's no other way. Simply digging about in cellars is useless and anyway illegal, according to §47a, subsection Y, Roman XXIII.'

And so it came about.

The suggestion put forward by one foreign engineer, too clever by half, that it would be wise to check whether Mackintosh might not have planted his gold himself at the places where it was found, in order to hoodwink the Commission, was dismissed with a condescending smile.

Such a hammering and crashing in the streets, rafters falling, workmen shouting, the rumble of rubble-carts, and everywhere that damned wind, blowing the dust about in clouds! It was enough to drive you mad.

The whole town was suffering from inflamed eyes: the waiting rooms of the ophthalmic clinic were bursting with patients crowding in, and a new pamphlet by Professor Weekly: *On the deleterious impact of modern building processes on the human cornea* was sold out in just a few days.

Things were getting worse.

Traffic was brought to a halt. Crowds besieged the 'Sun', all trying to speak to the American, to ask if he didn't think there was bound to be gold under other buildings besides those mentioned in the plan. Military patrols made their appearance, official proclamations were pasted up on all street corners announcing that it was strictly forbidden to pull down any more houses before ministerial permission had been granted.

The police appeared conspicuously armed: it had hardly any effect. News of dreadful cases of mental derangement started to circulate. In the suburbs a widow had climbed onto her roof in her nightdress and started to tear down the tiles, shrieking all the while.

Young mothers staggered along the streets as if drunk; poor abandoned babes lay parched and withered in lonely rooms.

A haze hung over all the city, dark, as if the demon Gold had spread his batwings over everything.

At last the great day came. The magnificent edifices of the past had vanished, as if torn out of the ground, and an army of miners had replaced the bricklayers.

Picks and shovels flashed.

But of gold — not a trace. It must lie deeper than had been supposed.

Then: there appeared a huge advertisement in the daily papers:

GEORGE MACKINTOSH TO HIS DEAR ACQUAINTANCES AND THE TOWN HE HAS GROWN SO FOND OF

Circumstances oblige me to say farewell to you all for ever. To the city I hereby donate the large captive balloon which you will see flying for the first time this afternoon from Joseph Square, and which may be used freely at any time in remembrance of me. I have found it difficult to make a final visit to everyone, so in lieu I leave in the town a *grand visiting card*.

'But that's absurd! To leave a visiting card in the *town*? Sheer nonsense! What can all that be about? Do you understand it?'

This was the cry on everyone's lips.

'It's odd that the American secretly sold all his property a week ago!'

It was the photographer Maloch who eventually shed some light on this riddle. He was the first to take a flight in the aforementioned balloon, and to have a bird's eye view of the urban devastation. His photograph of the scene was displayed in his shop window. The street was full of eager onlookers.

What did they see?

The white rubble of the empty building plots shone out clearly from among the dark sea of houses, outlining a jagged flourish:

$$> >G.M< <$$

The American's initials!

For most of the property owners the blow was a shattering one, but it made no odds to the old broker Schlüsselbein. His house had been falling down anyway. He just rubbed his reddened eyes angrily and growled: 'I always said so - Mackintosh never had a mind for anything serious.'

WETHERGLOBIN

I

Motto: Dulce et decorum est pro - patria mori.

The rumour ran from mouth to mouth, from newspaper to newspaper: Professor Domitian Dredrebaisel, the world-famous bacteriologist, had made a scientific discovery of quite stupendously far-reaching consequence.

The general opinion was that a reorganisation of the military was expected; oh yes, indeed, perhaps even a complete transformation of the armed services as we knew them. Why else would the Minister of War have been in such a hurry to summon the famous scientist to a meeting? Hm?

And once it was known that secret stock-market syndicates had been set up to exploit the discovery and to advance Professor Dredrebaisel a large sum of money so that he could undertake an urgent study trip to Borneo (Borneo?!), there was no end of popping eyes and wagging jaws.

'But I ask you, could we bring Borneo to the War Ministry?' Herr Galizenstein, that respected stockbroker, and relative of the scientist, had replied amid gesticulations, when interviewed on the subject. 'How could we bring Borneo to the War Ministry?! Where is Borneo, anyway?'

The following day the newspapers repeated every charming syllable of the words of our far-sighted financier, adding that an American government expert, Mr. G. R. S. Slyfox, M.D., F.R.S., had just had an audience with Professor Dredrebaisel.

All of which, of course, raised public curiosity to fever pitch.

Newshawks used to bribe the clerks in the War Ministry to find out details of new inventions that had been submitted; in the course of their activities they would repeatedly unearth material that bore eloquent witness to man's cease-less endeavours to perfect the science of warfare. Very innovative in the opinion of experts, was, for example, a proposed submission regarding the operation of the bag-gage train in both war and manoeuvres that would improve the current success rate of nought percent by five (!) times.

But the *pièce de résistance*, all were agreed, was the ingenious Automatic Honour Calibrator invented by Infan-try Captain Gustav Braidiner, an officer who was famous far beyond the borders of our country for his uncommonly idiosyncratic conception of the word of honour. Just imagine, an appliance, a clockwork mechanism that any lieutenant can operate without previous experience or in-struction, in brief a power-driven, water-cooled officer's code of honour which can be aimed in any direction at a touch: it does away with all the lengthy and tedious coaching in the prescribed honourable attitude for each individual situation, replacing it with a hygienic mechanical device.

Many, many such things came to light, but there was no trace of any invention or discovery by Professor Dredrebai-sel.

So there was nothing for it but to be patient, to let matters ripen like fruit on the trees, and wait for the results of the expedition to Borneo.

Months passed.

All the rumours of the great invention had long since nodded off and left the field to new questions, when a European newspaper broke the news that Professor Dredrebaisel, and with him perhaps all his companions, had died a terrible death. All that was known was contained in a brief telegram:

13th May. Silindong, Pakpak District, Borneo.
(A cable from our own correspondent.)

'Last night Professor Domitian Dredrebaisel was torn to pieces in his own house by a horde of orang-utans. Many servants and keepers shared his fate. His assistant, Dr. Slyfox, is missing. The Professor's desk was smashed; the floor was covered with countless scraps of paper from his notes and articles.'

A brief obituary for a glorious idea.

II

Motto:

Rear ends covered with brass buttons, fill turkey-cocks with pride.
And what makes them even prouder: they think with their backsides.

A letter written three years later from Borneo by a certain Dr. Ipse to a friend:

Silindong,
Borneo,

1st April 1906.

My dear old friend,

Do you remember – years ago in Maader's 'Box' it was – how we promised each other we would write at once if, in the course of our journey through life, we should ever come across anything which was beyond the experience of the common herd, anything which had an air of the extraordinary, the mysterious about it, anything, in short, which did not fit in with the banal merry-go-round of daily life?

Well, old chap, today I am in the happy position of being able to report something of the kind, something which justifies taking you away from your alchemical tomes or whatever recondite studies you are immersed in at the moment.

How will you feel, over there in Europe, if someone from far-away Borneo should dare to use the axe of knowledge to attack your unbounded awe of all things military at its roots?

I would love to be able to eavesdrop on your thoughts for a while after you have read this letter, to see how soon it was before your patriotism had been washed clean of all pride in the uniform, just as the message written in sugar is washed from a gingerbread soldier that has been left out in the rain.

Tell me, have you never wondered why it is that educated people of the same profession – yes, even barbers – call each other 'colleagues' (which in English means 'people who read or study together'), whilst the turkey-cocks who form our officer class address each other as 'comrade' (from *camera* = room = to sleep or lounge around in the same room)? It always reminds me of a nice chapter heading used by the medieval scholar, van Helmont, 'Of divers profound Mysteries that do lie in Words and Phrases.'

But now I must plunge head first into the whirlpool of events.

First of all, guess whom I met here? None other than Mr. G. R. S. Slyfox, M.D., F.R.S., former assistant to the late, lamented Professor Dredrebaisel. Just imagine! Here in Silindong, in the deepest jungle in Borneo! Mr. Slyfox was the only survivor of that ill-fated expedition. In reality it was he who had directed the experiment from the very beginning, Professor D.D. was only the front man, and immediately after the Professor's death he left Borneo for Europe to offer the perfected version of his discovery, or rather, invention, to several states, above all to the one we all love and admire so much which had shown such great initial interest.

I will come to the success of his trip later. For the moment suffice it to say that Mr. Slyfox is back in Silindong, poor as a church mouse and continuing his researches.

And now, I assume, you are impatient to know what Professor D.'s, or rather, Mr. Slyfox' invention actually consists of.

Admit it. You are, aren't you? Well then:

In decades of studying the inoculation statistics Mr. Slyfox had observed that, in areas where the smallpox vaccine was no longer taken from humans but from calves, there was a marked increase in the urge to defend the fatherland, even when there was not the slightest necessity.

In Mr. Slyfox' inventive mind it was only one step from this observation to his later, epoch-making experiments.

With the unerring judgment of an American, for whom nothing is sacred, he immediately connected the above-mentioned symptom with the inferior mental capacity of calves, and this provided the basis for a series of experiments.

His very first tests, using a number of specially selected surgically treated rams (those that are normally called 'wethers'), produced outstanding results. And if, in addition, the vaccine derived from such wethers (so-called Wetherglobin A) was passed through the blood stream of one or two sloths, it became so effective that, when injected into youths with a natural low patriotism quotient, it produced a kind of primary patriotic frenzy within a very short time.

In individuals with a hereditary tendency to patriotism, this state rapidly developed into incurable, galloping patrio-mania.

The profound changes that were also brought about in the aesthetic sensibilities of the inoculee can perhaps best be demonstrated by the case of one of our most respected cavalry poets who, after inoculation, opened his volume of poems with the lines:

O blade at my left side – aah,
A-gleaming as a I ride – aah.
etc., etc.

But to return to Mr. Slyfox: initially, as you will be aware, the government was extremely interested in the invention, which was to be put out under Professor Dredrebaisel's name, and a syndicate had advanced the costs of the expedition.

Silindong, in the middle of the most impenetrable jungle of Borneo, is the home of the orang-utan, and as quickly as possible around two hundred such apes were captured and immediately injected with Wetherglobin simplex A.

Mr. Slyfox maintained that the enrichment with lymphatic secretions, which came from passing the substance through sloths, would be, given the rarity of these animals, much too expensive for its mass use in the armed forces. He hoped that the characteristic of the sloth which produced the strengthening of the vaccine – its surplus stupidity – could be replaced, perhaps even improved, by the great ape's innate qualities.

Of course, no one could have foreseen the fateful consequences of locking up so many strong animals together.

The night of terror, in the course of which the orangutans smashed their cages, and everthing else, to smithereens and killed Professor D.D. and their Malay keepers, almost cost Mr. Slyfox his life too; it was only by a miracle that he escaped.

After they had finished destroying the camp, the orangutans held a meeting lasting several days, the purpose of which was at first a complete mystery but later highlighted the effects of Wetherglobin and everything connected with it.

From his hiding place the American had been able to observe how the apes, after endless palaver, had chosen one of the group as leader – it was the one which, even when they were imprisoned, had struck everybody as being completely gaga – and had then taken some gold (!) paper they had found in a broken box and stuck it on its backside.

The scene which then gradually unrolled before the American's eyes was equally calculated to arouse amazement.

The orang-utans formed up in platoons with sticks and branches, or whatever they could get hold of, over their shoulders, and set off, marching upright in close formation along the jungle paths, with their leader, gold backside gleaming and full of his own importance, a short distance in front. From time to time he would bark out:

'Gwaaah-gwek! Gwaaah-gwek!'

which would send them all into a kind of black ecstasy.

An oddly grumpy expression would come over their features, they would jerk their faces to the left and stamp the ground with their heels like maniacs as they marched.

It must have been an unforgettable sight. 'For a few moments,' these were Mr. Slyfox' own words, 'I felt I was no longer in the jungle, but somewhere quite different, on some parade ground in Europe.'

And later, when I saw how an objector was arrested and one of the apes stood on a leather hat-box and gave such a deafening performance that eventually even this stubborn individualist was seized by 'primary patriotic fervour', well, the new ideas came simply flooding in.

These apes, so I reasoned, have nothing to model themselves on, and yet they have come up with the idea of decorating their rear ends with gold to make a warlike impression, and they have hit upon institutions which, in the light of my research I now know must be the result of the effect of substances similar to Wetherglobin clouding the brain, whether injected or produced by the body itself, where their development is encouraged by hereditary bigotry.

I will deliberately refrain, my dear old friend, from taking Slyfox' train of thought any farther, if for no other reason than so as not to deny you the subtle pleasure of working it out for yourself.

And would you not have to agree with me if I were to maintain that the arrogance of the turkey-cocks has nothing to do with true patriotism and everything to do with the desire to impress 'harlots' of both sexes, with a kind of capercaillie's courtship display?

Or is it really possible that two such as us, whose friendship has weathered into a union of souls, could have different opinions on such a fundamental truth, even for a fraction of a second?

And even if that were the case, would it not really be sufficient to call to mind the average level of culture of the 'turkey-cocks'; of course, I am thinking of those of a particular great power.

But away with such speculation. I was going to tell you what the attitudes of those states was to whom Mr. Slyfox offered Wetherglobin.

One gave a curt refusal; they wanted to observe the effect in other countries first.

The other replied, informally through an intermediary as usual, to the effect that, thanks to the traditional loyalty to the royal family, to quotations and patriotic songs learnt off by heart at an early age, as well as to cleverly designed and brightly coloured children's toys etc., the vast majority of its population was already in a satisfactory condition. A programme of vaccination such as the one proposed, especially since it was no longer guaranteed by the name of the unfortunate Professor Dredrebaisel, seemed, therefore, premature. Added to that, in the opinion of experts it had not been conclusively proved that Wetherglobin would not, like other toxins, after some time lead to the production of antitoxins in the blood which would have the opposite effect.

They would, however, naturally continue to follow Mr. Slyfox' experiments with keen interest and remained, etc., etc. So Mr. Slyfox was left high and dry and had no choice but to continue his experiments on all kinds of beasts over here.

And I'm assisting him.

Even if, contrary to expectation, success has so far eluded us, we are determined to catch a rhinoceros and inject it with Wetherglobin. That is certain – Mr. Slyfox would bet his bottom dollar on it – to convince all the sceptics.

By the way, old chap, I meant to say that the apes are no danger to us any more, just in case you were concerned for my safety. We too have decorated our backsides with tinsel and, as long as we are careful to suppress any sign of intelligence when the animals approach, they take us for officers and treat us with great respect, so that we are completely safe. You might feel that shows a certain lack of principle, but there are some concessions you have to make if you live among orang-utans.

But I'll have to finish quickly now, outside I can hear the patriotic apes approaching with their smart

'Gwaaah-gwek! Gwaaah-gwek!'

Hearty but hasty greetings from your old friend,

Egon Ipse.

translated by Mike Mitchell

The Translators

Maurice Raraty was a senior lecturer in German at the University of Kent, with an interest also in Comparative Literature. He has published various studies on the work of E. T. A. Hoffman and has translated a wide variety of texts from German.

He has compiled and translated *The Short Stories of Gustav Meyrink Volume I (The Opal and other stories)* for Dedalus.

Mike Mitchell has translated the story *Wetherglobin* for *The Short Stories of Gustav Meyrink Volume I (The Opal and other stories)* and has compiled and translated *The Short Stories of Gustav Meyrink Volume II (The Master and other stories)*.

He will shortly publish his one hundredth translation from German and French.

Books by and about Gustav Meyrink which are available
from Dedalus

The five novels translated by Mike Mitchell:

The Golem
The Angel of the West Window
The Green Face
Walpurgisnacht
The White Domican

A two-volume collection of short stories. *Volume I (The Opal
and other stories)* translated by Maurice Raraty and *Volume II
(The Master and other stories)* translated by Mike Mitchell.

A sampler for Gustav Meyrink's complete works edited and
translated by Mike Mitchell:

The Dedalus Meyrink Reader

The first English language biography of Gustav Meyrink
written by Mike Mitchell:

Vivo: The Life of Gustav Meyrink